GOBBO THE GREAT

HAPPY HUNDREDTH BIRTHDAY, BENNETT SCHOOL!

Somehow Barny and Spag and Clipper have to prove to Thrasher Dyson and the other jeering members of the rival school that Bennett School is not an old dump. When it comes to celebrating a hundred years they decide to let people peep into the twenty-first century . . .

Also by Gillian Cross
available from Methuen Children's Books
and Mammoth Books

SAVE OUR SCHOOL★
THE MINTYGLO KID
SWIMATHON★

RESCUING GLORIA
★available from Mammoth only

GILLIAN CROSS

GOBBO THE GREAT

Illustrated by Philippe Dupasquier

MAMMOTH

First published in Great Britain 1991
by Methuen Children's Books Ltd
Published 1991 by Mammoth
an imprint of Mandarin Paperbacks
Michelin House, 81 Fulham Road, London SW3 6RB

Mandarin is an imprint of the Octopus Publishing Group,
a division of Reed International Books Ltd

ISBN 0 7497 0605 8

Text copyright © 1991 Gillian Cross
Illustrations copyright © 1991 Philippe Dupasquier

A CIP catalogue record for this title
is available from the British Library

Printed in Great Britain
by Cox & Wyman Ltd, Reading, Berkshire

Contents

1

The Next Hundred Years!

'Bennett School is falling down,
Falling down, falling down,
Bennett School is falling down –
HA! HA! HA!'

The song hit Barny and Spag and Clipper right between the eyes as they came round the corner. There was Thrasher Dyson lounging against the school gatepost, grinning at them.

'Hurry up!' he jeered. 'The old dump might fall down before you get inside.'

'It's not an old dump!' said Clipper fiercely. 'It's much better than your boring school. That's all glass and concrete.'

Thrasher snorted. 'At least King's Road's modern. Not out of date, like this old ruin.'

He waved a hand at the metal arch over the gate. For the first time, Barny and Spag and Clipper looked up. A big white banner was draped across the arch, and bold black letters stretched from side to side.

HAPPY 100TH BIRTHDAY BENNETT SCHOOL!

Over the main entrance there was another banner, even bigger, lettered in red.

BENNETT SCHOOL – 100 YEARS OLD THIS TERM!!

'It's older than my grandad,' Thrasher said scornfully. 'How can you learn anything modern in a place like *that*?'

Spag blinked at him. 'At least it's not a goldfish bowl, like King's Road.'

'They hadn't invented glass when this place

8

was built!' Thrasher said. 'They were all running round in skins with stone axes.'

Clipper clenched her fists. 'You – '

Spag frowned. 'Stone axes were more than a hundred years ago – '

But Barny didn't let either of them finish. He grabbed Spag's arm with one hand and Clipper's with the other and dragged them both towards the school gate. Mrs Rumbelow was coming down the road towards them. It wasn't a good idea to start a fight with Thrasher.

Clipper was furious. 'He'll think we're running away. He'll think we're *scared*.'

'Doesn't matter what he thinks,' Barny said. 'Does it, Spag?'

But Spag was looking worried. 'It might. If the teachers go on and on about how old this school is, people *will* think it's out of date.'

'So?' Barny shrugged. 'I don't care what people think.'

'You will,' Spag said gloomily. 'If they stop coming here. If we don't get enough children, the school will close. And we'll have to go to King's Road. With Thrasher.'

He frowned up at the red and white banner as they walked through the front door. And he was still frowning when they all went into the hall for assembly.

'You wait,' he muttered. 'I bet the Head Mister goes on and on about how *old* the school is.'

'It'll be OK,' Barny whispered as they sat down. 'After all – '

But he didn't have time to finish. At that moment, a loud, ferocious voice boomed from behind them.

'Silence!'

Everyone stopped talking, all over the hall. They turned round to see who had shouted, and when they did see there was a long, loud gasp.

'Look!' whispered Clipper.

It was the Head. But he didn't look like himself at all. He came marching down the middle of the hall, glaring from side to side instead of smiling. Over his normal clothes he had a long black gown, and he carried a cane in his right hand. As he walked, he swished it up and down.

Barny pulled a face. 'The Head Mister's gone mad,' he muttered.

'Sssh!' hissed Clipper. But it was too late. The Head stopped. Very slowly, he turned and looked along the row of children, until his eyes reached Barny.

'Gobbo!' he roared in a terrible voice. 'Did I hear you *speak*?'

Barny blinked. 'I only – '

The Head took a deep breath and roared even more loudly. 'Stand up when you talk to me, boy!'

Barny stared at him.

'Stand *up*!'

As Barny scrambled to his feet, Soppy Elaine Potter, who was sitting behind him, gave a loud giggle. He turned round, to stick his tongue out at her, and fell over Spag's leg. Elaine yelped as his foot landed on her knee.

'Sir! *Sir*! Gobbo *trod* on me!'

'COME HERE, GOBBO!'

Barny clambered over all the legs, to the end of the row. The Head grabbed his ear and marched him down the middle of the hall and on to the platform. Swishing the cane in the air again, he glared round at the other children.

'Well?' he bellowed. 'Has anyone got anything to say?'

Nobody said a word. Nobody moved.

'Nothing at all?'

The hall was completely silent, except for the swish of the cane.

And then, slowly, a smile crept across the Head's face. 'Hasn't *anyone* noticed anything peculiar?'

Barny looked up at him and saw that he was trying not to laugh.

'*I've* noticed something peculiar,' he said. 'You're pulling my ear off.'

The Head's smile turned into a great, beaming grin. 'Well done, Gobbo! And *why* do you think I'm pulling your ear off?'

'Because you've gone mad, sir?'

The Head's grin didn't change. 'No, Gobbo, I haven't gone mad. What am I doing?'

Down in the hall, a hand shot up. It was Spag's. 'You're pretending it's a hundred years ago,' he said gloomily.

'That's *right*!' The Head chuckled. 'Gobbo wouldn't have been allowed to talk in assembly then. Would he?'

Barny started to shake his head, but that was a mistake. His ear nearly came off.

'You'd have got worse than that a hundred • years ago,' the Head said cheerfully. 'What would it have been?'

Spotty McGrew's hand shot up. 'Please, sir! Six of the best. With the cane.'

'Excellent!' The Head beamed again and swished the cane. Barny looked nervously at it.

'You can't *do* that!' Clipper said, jumping

to her feet. 'Teachers can't beat up children whenever they want. Not now.'

'Of course they can't. Very good, Clipper.' The Head dropped the cane. 'That's one thing that's changed in the last hundred years. What other changes can you think of?'

For a moment no one moved. Then Spag's hand went up again. 'Computers, sir. They didn't have computers a hundred years ago. Or aeroplanes. Or cars or videos or – '

' – or My Little Pony,' Soppy Elaine said. 'Or Sindy dolls, or Barbie, or – '

'Or American football!' shouted Spotty McGrew.

'Or McDonalds – '

'Or television – '

Everyone was joining in now, all of them shouting at once. The Head held up his hands for silence.

'You've all got the idea. In the last hundred years, *most* things have changed, haven't they?'

'I know two things that haven't!' shouted Spotty McGrew.

Everyone turned to look at him.

'Yes?' said the Head. 'And what are those?'

'Gobbo's socks!'

'That's not true!' Barny shouted. 'I change my socks every day! Not like you! You wore those red socks with the holes in for a whole *week*.'

'That's a lie!'

'Oh no it's not!'

'Be quiet! Both of you!' The Head pushed Barny towards the steps. 'Sometimes I think things were *better* a hundred years ago! Go and sit down, Gobbo.'

Barny slid into his place between Spag and Clipper.

Spag was looking even gloomier than before. 'You see?' he whispered. 'They'll be going on about *a hundred years ago* until we're sick of it. And everyone will think this place is an old ruin. Just like Thrasher says.'

But the Head was taking off his black gown. He rubbed his hands together and looked all round the hall.

'Now then. You've told me a lot about the changes in the last hundred years. But we don't want people to think this is a fuddy-duddy, old-fashioned school. We don't want them to think we're living in the past, do we? So – '

He stopped for a second and grinned down at everyone. When they were all completely silent, he leaned forward.

'*What about the NEXT hundred years?*'

'It's brilliant!' Spag said as they went back to their classroom. His frown had vanished and he was almost bouncing up and down. 'It's absolutely *brilliant*!'

'But I don't get it,' said Barny. 'What does he want us to do?'

'A project, dimbo.' Clipper flopped into her chair and leaned back with a grin. 'A really *modern* project. That'll fix Thrasher.'

'But how – ?'

'It's more than modern,' Spag interrupted. 'It's about the future.'

'But how can we know what's going to happen in the future?' said Barny.

'You *guess*, pinhead,' said Clipper.

'You work it out,' said Spag.

'By imagination.'

'Scientifically.'

Their voices had risen as they got more and more excited. Up at the front of the classroom, Mr Fox banged his hand on the desk.

'Have you three finished? Can I explain to the whole class now?'

He waited until Barny, Spag and Clipper had turned round, and then he went on.

'You're all going to do a project. About what the world will be like in a hundred years' time. All the projects will be on show on Anniversary Day, which is the school's actual birthday. And the exhibition will be open to the public.'

Soppy Elaine's eyes lit up. 'Oooh, *sir!*'

'You can do any kind of project,' Mr Fox said. 'And there'll be a prize for the best one.'

Soppy Elaine was already whispering to

Sharon Grove. When Mr Fox said *a prize*, her hand shot up.

'Me and Sharon are going to do Fashions of the Future, sir,' she announced loudly. 'We're going to work out what we'll all be wearing, and how the teachers will dress, and what the new colours will be and – '

'Very good, Elaine,' Mr Fox said. 'Has anyone else got an idea yet?'

'How about slang, sir?' said Spotty. 'That changes, doesn't it? Could I do a slang dictionary for a hundred years ahead?'

'Excellent!' Mr Fox grinned. 'You can have some fun with that.'

Elaine sniffed. 'It won't have pictures though, will it? Me and Sharon are going to do loads and loads of pictures for our project – '

'A project doesn't have to have pictures,' Spotty said. 'Does it, sir?'

'Pictures are better, though,' Elaine tossed her head. 'Pictures are more interesting and they help you to understand things – '

'Interesting? Pictures of rotten old dresses?' Spotty laughed sarcastically and Elaine's bottom lip trembled.

Mr Fox sighed. 'That's enough, you two. People don't want to hear about your projects. They want to plan their own. Get into groups, all of you, and decide what you're going to do.'

Clipper grabbed Barny and Spag and hauled them into a corner.

17

'I've got this really brilliant idea!' she hissed. 'I think we ought to do a newspaper. From a hundred years ahead. With articles and photographs and – '

'Bor*ing*.' Spag pulled a face. 'That's the sort of thing teachers think up. I want to do something *serious*. A proper scientific report on the environment. With diagrams and graphs and – '

'Diagrams? Graphs?' Clipper made sick noises. 'Honestly, Spag, you haven't got a clue.'

Spag looked annoyed. 'I can't see the point of just making things up – '

'And I can't see the point of being dull!' said Clipper. 'What's the use of a scientific report that no one reads? Our project's got to have zap!'

'Zap?' said Spag. 'What's zap? We want to do something *valuable*. To impress people. So they'll send their children here.'

'Your idea's more likely to send them to sleep!' Clipper said. She turned to Barny. 'Come on, Gobbo. You haven't said a word yet. Don't *you* think we ought to do a newspaper?'

'If you do, I won't be in your group.' Spag folded his arms stubbornly. 'I've done loads of fake newspapers and I'm sick of them. I want to do a project that's worth something.'

'Well, I'm not doing a scientific report,'

snapped Clipper. 'I know what that means.
You'd make us read lots of books that no one
understands except you.'

She folded her arms too, and they turned
away from each other and glared at Barny.

'Who are you going to be with?' Clipper
said. 'Me or Spag?'

Barny looked from one to the other. 'But
you can't do different things. We always do
projects together.'

'You think of another idea then,' said Spag.
'If you're so clever. Because I'm not doing
Clipper's.'

'And I'm not doing his!'

It was the worst row they had ever had.
Barny didn't know what to do. If he chose
Clipper's project, Spag would go off by him-
self. And if he chose Spag's Clipper would

never speak to him again. If only he had an idea of his own . . .

'Well?' said Spag. 'What are you going to do?'

'I – I – ' Barny thought quickly. 'Why don't you each do a sample? Then we can look at them both after school.'

'Hmmph,' said Clipper.

'Well – maybe,' said Spag.

That was the last time they spoke to him until the end of school. They both spent every free moment scribbling furiously. When the time came to go home, each of them had pages and pages of writing.

'Wait till you read this!' Clipper waved her untidy bundle of paper as they walked out of school. 'It's sensational!'

Spag stroked the cover of his ring binder. 'Not as good as mine. I've planned the whole report, in seventeen chapters.'

'*Seventeen*! No one's going to read all those – '

'*Some* people can read more than three words at a time – '

Barny sighed. Were they going to quarrel all the way home?

But before they got really cross, Thrasher came strolling round the corner. He smirked when he saw them.

'Well, look who it isn't. The mouldy oldies

from the Bennett.' At the top of his voice, he started to recite:

'Bennett School is old and useless,
Take it to the tip.
If you go to Bennett School,
You must be a drip!'

'And I suppose you're great, just because you go to King's Road.' Barny snorted. 'Wait till you see what we're doing this term. It'll make you wish you were at our school.'

'Me? At the Bennett?' Thrasher fell about laughing.

'People will be fighting to come here,' said Spag. 'Once they've seen our Exhibition. It's going to be really up to date and – and – full of zap!'

Thrasher sneered. 'Take more than an exhibition to get *me* into that old ruin.'

'It won't be an ordinary exhibition,' Clipper said. 'It's going to be really interesting. And exciting. And – and *valuable*.'

'Valuable?' Thrasher stopped smirking and looked sharply at them. 'What d'you mean, "valuable?"'

There was a greedy, suspicious gleam in his eyes. *Valuable* meant only one thing to Thrasher – money.

Barny winked at the other two. 'We're

going to have something *really valuable* for the exhibition,' he said. 'Aren't we, Clipper?'

Clipper nodded solemnly. 'That's right. It's going to be *worth an awful lot*. Isn't it, Spag?'

'Sssh!' hissed Spag, mysteriously.

Thrasher goggled at them. 'You're having me on. Who's going to let *you* have really valuable things? You're only kids.'

'No one's going to let us have them,' Spag said. 'They'll be things we've discovered. All by ourselves.'

'Discovered?' Thrasher's eyes were like saucers. 'What have you discovered? Gold? Jewels? Money?'

'Wait and see,' Clipper said sweetly.

She side-stepped neatly round him and walked off up the road. Thrasher turned to Spag and Barny.

'What's she on about? What are you up to?'

'Think we're telling anyone from King's Road? If you're so great, you can find out for yourself.' Barny grabbed Spag's arm and pulled him away. He had to escape before he burst out laughing.

He didn't see Thrasher staring after them. Watching thoughtfully as they ran off towards the big gates that said J. F. GOBBO. SECONDHAND FURNITURE. HOUSES CLEARED.

2

FutureScope!

The three of them were splitting with laughter as they ran into the scrapyard. But it didn't last long. The moment they were in Barny's house, Clipper and Spag began to argue about the project again.

'This is the sort of thing we need!' Clipper waved her papers at Spag. 'Listen to this:

IS THE WORLD REALLY GETTING WARMER?
WHAT WILL HAPPEN WHEN THE ICE CAPS MELT??
Top scientists predict . . .'

Spag was reading over her shoulder. 'That's no good. It's just chatter. You haven't got any facts at all.'

'Yes I have!' Clipper said fiercely. She leafed through her papers, dropped half of them on the ground and snatched one up. 'What about this?' She read it out at the top of her voice:

'BENNETT SCHOOL IN DANGER!!!
When the world gets warmer, ice will melt and the oceans will get fuller. Lots of low-lying places could be flooded.
INCLUDING BENNETT SCHOOL!!!!
In less than thirty years, our classroom could be full of WATER!!'

'That's just scaremongering.' Spag opened his file and flipped through the pages of neat notes. '*This* is how it should be done.'

He held out the file so that Barny and Clipper could see the list of chapters.

'*Chapter 1 – *' Barny read. '*A history of past weather.*

'*Chapter 2 – The causes of global warming.*

'*Chapter 3 – Likely effects of global warming . . .*'

'That's where the school comes in,' Spag said. 'We'll have graphs to show how the water level would rise. And charts to show which places are most in danger – '

'Yawn, yawn, *yawn*!' Clipper put her hand in front of her mouth. 'We don't want all that junk. Do we, Gobbo?'

'I – um – '

'Come on, Gobbo.' Spag turned round to look at Barny. 'It's time to say what you think. It's pretty obvious which is the best project.'

'That's *right*!' Clipper said. 'It's mine. Isn't it?'

Barny looked at Spag's angry, stubborn face and then at Clipper's. *Help*! he thought. *How do I get out of this one*?

As if by magic, his mother appeared in the kitchen doorway.

'Who wants toasted teacakes?' she said.

Clipper stopped glaring at Barny and turned round to grin at Mrs Gobbo. 'Toasted teacakes! Yum! Scrum! They're my favourite!'

'You want any?' Mrs Gobbo said, to Spag's back.

Spag shut his folder with a snap. 'Yes please. If it's not too much trouble.'

'No trouble to *me*,' Mrs Gobbo said. 'You can toast them yourselves if you want them.'

Thirty seconds later, Spag and Clipper were in the kitchen, toasting teacakes together as if they had never disagreed in their lives.

Mrs Gobbo settled down at the kitchen table. 'Come and give us a hand then, Barny. While the other two are cooking.'

She was having one of her massive shoe-cleaning sessions, with fifteen pairs of shoes lined up on sheets of newspaper. She handed Barny the polishing cloth and his father's best black shoes.

When he was rubbing away at them, she looked up. 'What was all that noise about?'

'I – er – ' Barny dropped the cloth. 'We were trying to choose our project. About life in a hundred years' time.'

'Project? You never said nothing about projects. Is it for a competition?'

'Not really. Well – sort of.' Barny suddenly remembered. 'There's a prize for the best one. And some people have got really good ideas. Spotty Mcgrew's doing a slang dictionary. Elaine Potter and Sharon Grove are doing twenty-first-century clothes – '

'Not interested in them.' Mrs Gobbo

26

picked up the red shoe brush. 'What about you three?'

'We – ' Barny stopped and stared at his fingers.

'Don't let me down, now.' His mother tapped the shoe brush on the table. 'That swanky Mrs Potter's always showing off about her Elaine. Be one in the eye for her if *you* got the prize.'

'Yes, but – ' Barny picked up Clipper's papers and Spag's folder and put them on the table. 'We don't know which of these to do.'

'Let's see.' Mrs Gobbo reached for the papers, leaving a large, red thumbprint on Spag's folder. She flicked through both sets of notes for a second and then pushed them aside.

'I can't plough through all that. Life's too short.'

'You've got to read more than *that*,' Barny said crossly. 'Or how are you going to know what we're talking about?'

'I want to *see* it all.' Mrs Gobbo looked thoughtful as she levered the lid off the red shoe polish. 'A peep into the future. That's what I'd like.'

'Oh great!' Barny pulled a face. 'We'll just build a time machine then.'

'No need to be cheeky.' Mrs Gobbo looked over at Spag and Clipper and raised her voice. 'How are you two getting on?'

'Brilliant.' Clipper picked up a plate full of teacakes that dripped butter.

'You're not eating *those* in my kitchen,' Mrs Gobbo said. 'Take them outside.'

'Aw, Mum!' Barny looked out at the yard. 'It's raining!'

'Find somewhere to shelter, then. I've just washed this floor, and I'm not having it covered in butter.'

'But we – '

'Out!'

Grumbling, Barny followed Clipper and Spag out of the house. It was much too wet to sit around. They'd have to find some kind of den.

He scanned the yard. There was an old tin bath, propped up by the gate . . . a pile of fireplaces . . . a heap of trays . . . and a wardrobe . . .

'Where are we going?' Clipper said impatiently. 'The teacakes are getting soggy.'

'OK, OK.' Barny thought it would have to be the wardrobe and the tin bath, pushed together. But he took one more look round the yard.

And that was when he saw it. The perfect place.

It was a huge old water tank, in the far corner of the yard. It must have come from a hospital or a hotel, because it was three or four times the normal size. Lying on its side, it made a kind of metal cave.

'Come on!' he said.

He led the way round chairs and past

fireplaces and the other two followed. Clipper muttered as she tried to keep the teacakes balanced.

'Honestly, Gobbo, why did you have to choose the farthest thing in the whole yard? These teacakes are getting really slippery.'

'Nearly there.'

Barny fell to his knees, crawled round to the back of the water tank and wriggled in. Inside, it was perfectly dry and there was room for all three of them.

'What a brilliant place!' Clipper stopped grumbling and wriggled in after him. 'No one would ever find us in here.'

'We could watch *them*, though.' Spag waved at the sides of the tank. Lots of short pieces of pipe stuck through the metal walls. 'Those are like telescopes. Or periscopes. If we keep a watch through them, we can see if anyone's creeping up on us.'

'Let's have a look.' Clipper pushed the plate of teacakes into Barny's hands and put one eye to a pipe hole. 'You're right! It's fabulous!' She clapped Spag on the back and he grinned at her.

Why can't they agree that easily about the project?' thought Barny. Absent-mindedly, he began to eat a teacake.

'Hey, Gobbo!' Clipper turned round and saw him. 'Stop guzzling. Don't you want a peep through here?'

A peep . . . Someone had said something about peeps earlier on. Who was it? It niggled at Barny's mind, but he couldn't quite remember.

'Yes, stop pigging out,' Spag said. He pointed at the pipes. 'Don't you want to see?'

A peep . . . *I want to see it* . . . Barny rubbed his eyes with a buttery hand. What was it that he couldn't quite remember?

He bent down and peered through the pipes in the back of the water tank. Spag and Clipper were right. They made beautiful peepholes.

He saw his mother come to the kitchen window and stare out for a moment or two, trying to see where they were.

He saw the dog from next door sniffing round the dustbin.

He saw –

Frowning, Barny peered harder through that pipe. He could see Thrasher Dyson outside the yard, peering craftily round the gatepost. What was he up to? He was obviously trying not to be seen. Should they go and take a look – ?

'Well?' said Clipper, breaking into his thoughts. 'Can you see it all?'

I want to see it all.

That was it!

Barny forgot about Thrasher's odd behaviour and a huge grin spread slowly across his

face. At last he'd realised what he was trying
to remember. It was what his mother had said
about the project. *I want to see it all. A peep
into the future. That's what I'd like.*

And he had just had the most stupendous
idea!

'Gobbo!'

'What's up with you?'

'Are you going to stand there for ever?'

'You're dropping the *teacakes!*'

Barny blinked, as if he had been dreaming.

Spag grabbed the plate of teacakes and looked hard at him.

'Are you all right?'

'Of course I'm all right.' Barny grinned. 'I'm a genius!'

'You're off your head,' said Clipper.

'No I'm not. I've just decided what to do for our project. And it's sensational. Much better than a newspaper. *Or* a scientific report.'

'Really?' Spag looked doubtful.

'Really,' said Barny. He took a deep breath. 'We're going to do something that no one's ever done before. In the whole world. We're going to build a – a FutureScope.'

'A what?' Clipper stared.

'A FutureScope.'

'You mean like – a telescope?' said Spag slowly.

'That's right. Only for looking at the future.' Barny waved a hand round the water tank, just missing Clipper's nose. 'See all these little bits of pipe sticking through the sides? They're the peepholes.'

'What use is that?' Clipper said. 'We can't see anything through those. Only the scrapyard.'

'But suppose they were different,' said Barny. 'Suppose the openings were covered by flaps. And the flaps said things like – "What will happen to Bennett School?" Or

"Where will electricity come from in a hundred years' time?" Then you lift the flap and you see – you see – '

He had no idea where electricity might come from in a hundred years' time. But Spag knew.

'A wind park,' he said dreamily. 'Rows and rows of windmills on top of a hill, all generating electricity whenever the wind blows. I'd love to see that.'

'But you *could*!' said Barny. 'All we have to do is make a model and fix it on the other side of the peephole, on the outside of the tank. Then when you lift the flap, it'll be like looking through a telescope at the future.'

'Hmm,' said Spag.

'It'll work!' Barny thumped his hand against the side of the tank. 'It will!'

'You know – it's not a bad idea.' Clipper grinned suddenly. 'And we'll have – ' she counted rapidly ' – twelve different models? One for each peephole?'

Barny nodded. 'They can all be about different things. That wind park of Spag's would make a good one. And we could do travel. And something about the world being warmer – '

'I know what to do for that!' Spag was beginning to look really interested. 'I've just been reading about it. There are scientists who want to fill the oceans with white ping-pong balls. To reflect the sun's heat away from the earth. We could make a fabulous model of that.'

'And trees!' Clipper grabbed Barny's arm. 'One of the labels could say, "What will be the worst crime in a hundred years' time?" We could have a gang of criminals in masks, trying to chop down trees. And policemen parachuting down to catch them.'

'There ought to be something about houses, too.' Spag tugged at Barny's other arm. 'In a hundred years' time they'll all have solar panels on the roof, to use the sun's heat – '

'And animals!' Clipper tugged too. 'Wild animals will all be protected. People might even have them as pets – '

'And we could make a model of a plate of food, to show what people will have for dinner – ' said Spag.

'And a model of the top pop group,' Clipper said, tugging Barny's arm again.

'Hey yes!' Spag almost yelled the words as he tugged too. 'We could do that one with *music*. So that a tape came on when the flap was lifted. That would be simple to do.'

'And – '

'HANG ON A MINUTE!' Barny wriggled free and shouted, as loudly as he could. 'You're pulling my arms off!'

'Don't be so boring, Gobbo!' Clipper let go of his elbow and shook her head at him.

'Why don't you think of something yourself, instead of whining?'

'That's right,' Spag said. 'If only you'd have a few ideas too – '

Barny nearly exploded. 'Who thought of the FutureScope in the first place? Me! I had the best idea of all. You're just filling in the details.'

'And they're *fabulous* details!' said Clipper. 'This is going to be the best thing in the whole Anniversary Day exhibition. Are you sure your dad will let us use the tank, Gobbo?'

'I – er – ' Barny hadn't got as far as thinking about that.

'He has to do more than let us use it,' said Spag. 'He'll have to take it to school for us. In his lorry.'

'OK. I'll ask him.' It was too soon to bother with details like that. Barny wanted to get on with the FutureScope. 'Why don't we start now?'

'We'll have to take a look at the outside of the tank,' Spag said. 'To see how to fix the models. And the flaps . . .'

Muttering to himself, he pulled out his pen and notebook and crawled out of the tank. Clipper gave Barny an impatient shove.

'Get moving. We've got lots to do.'

She shoved again and Barny toppled sideways, out of the tank. Clipper scrambled over him and went to look at Spag's notebook.

The first page was already covered with little diagrams.

'We'll have to put the models in boxes,' Spag said. He frowned. 'But I don't know how to fix them to the tank.'

'Use plastic bottles,' Clipper said briskly. 'The big ones that squash comes in. We can slip the necks of the bottles into the pipes and tape them on.'

'That's no good,' Barny said. 'How can we get models into bottles?'

Clipper looked pityingly at him. 'We cut off the bottoms of the bottles, of course. And stick them on again afterwards.'

'Yes, that should work.' Spag's eyes glittered. 'Plastic bottles will let in light, as well. But can we get hold of twelve of them in time?'

'I think we've got enough,' Barny said. 'My dad saves them for his homemade beer. Hang on a minute.'

He raced into the house. Spag and Clipper heard loud rattlings and clatterings coming from somewhere inside. Then Barny came very carefully through the kitchen door, trying to balance twelve empty plastic bottles at once.

'Be careful,' Clipper called. 'We want them in the water tank, not all over the yard. Shall I come and help?'

Barny peered round the heap of bottles, to

see where she was — and saw something else instead. Something very strange indeed.

The old tin bath wasn't leaning against the gatepost any more. It was lying upside down, halfway across the yard.

And it was moving.

Very slowly, like a giant robot tortoise, it was creeping nearer to Spag and Clipper.

3

Keeping the Secret

'C-Clipper – S-Spag – I – ulp – er – LOOK!'
    Barny gulped, yelped, wobbled – and tripped over a pile of flowerpots. Plastic bottles showered into the air and came rattling down all round him.

'What are you playing at?' yelled Clipper. 'You'll ruin them.'

'Don't be daft. Look!' Barny scrambled to his feet and pointed to the tin bath.

But it had stopped moving. It lay very still, upside down, next to the fireplaces.

'What's so special about that?' Spag said. 'It's just a lump of old metal.'

'But – but – ' Barny didn't want to say it out loud. He ploughed through the empty bottles and whispered the last two words close to Spag's ear. '*It moved.*'

'It what?' Spag stared at the bath again. 'Don't be soft, Gobbo. That's impossible.'

'But it *did*,' Barny insisted. 'I saw it.'

'What did what?' Clipper was getting impatient. 'Why are you two wasting time?'

'Barny said – ' Spag began.

'Ssh!' hissed Barny.

Spag pulled a face and turned away to whisper the rest in Clipper's ear.

The moment his back was turned, the bath slid a little closer.

'It did it again!' hissed Barny.

Spag and Clipper whirled round, but the bath was still again.

Clipper shook her head. 'You've finally gone over the top, Gobbo. You're seeing things.'

But Spag didn't look so sure. He studied the bath with his head on one side and then he looked round at the other two. *Wait*, he mouthed, putting his finger to his lips.

For a moment Clipper looked as if she wanted to argue. But then she changed her mind and stood like the others, perfectly still, staring at the bath.

The traffic was noisy outside, but it was very quiet in the yard. Nobody spoke. Nothing moved. Barny's nose began to itch but he didn't even scratch it, because he was so busy concentrating on the bath.

He had just decided that Clipper was right, and he had imagined the whole thing, when it happened again. The bath lifted slightly off the ground and slid another few paces towards them.

'Aha!' said Clipper.

In two strides, she was across the yard. She grabbed the bath by one of its handles and lifted it high into the air.

And there was a familiar figure, curled up on the ground.

'Well, well, well,' said Spag. 'The Great Thrasher Dyson. What are *you* doing here?'

Thrasher uncoiled himself and glared defiantly at them. 'I've come to see all these *valuable things* you were going on about.'

Clipper stared. 'But that was only a joke. We haven't really got anything valuable.'

'No good trying to put me off. I've worked out what's going on, haven't I?' Thrasher smirked craftily and tapped his head. 'Brains.'

'Really?' Spag blinked at him. 'What *is* going on, then?'

'Obvious, isn't it?' Thrasher said scornfully. 'Your lousy old school's a hundred years old, and you've got something valuable for the exhibition. Only one thing it can be.'

They were all staring at him now. 'What?' said Barny.

Thrasher looked triumphant. 'Antiques!'

'*Antiques*?' said Spag. 'Where would we get antiques from?'

Thrasher looked even more triumphant. 'Found them here, didn't you? In the yard. Bet there's stacks of valuable stuff rotting away in here. You've collected it up and stacked it in that tank of yours – '

'Don't be stupid!' It was all Barny could do not to burst out laughing. 'D'you think my dad would leave anything valuable – '

Thrasher suddenly stopped smirking and looked ferocious. 'DON'T TRY FOOLING ME, I SAID! My uncle's got an antique shop. And he's found loads of valuable stuff in yards like this. So I'm going to take a look – '

He put his head down and charged towards them. Clipper clenched her fists, but Barny and Spag grabbed her, because fighting Thrasher was bad news, even if you won. Anyone who beat Thrasher got a visit from Thrasher's brother Tiny. And there was nothing tiny about Tiny Dyson. He was as big as a bus.

But it wasn't so easy to put Clipper off. As Thrasher reached her, she stepped sideways, into his way, so that he had to swerve. He staggered to the right and cannoned into a stack of metal shelves.

With a noise like thunder, they cascaded to the ground and a second later the kitchen window flew open and Mrs Gobbo's head appeared.

When she saw Thrasher, standing in the middle of the slithering shelves, she turned bright red.

'ALAN DYSON! WHAT ARE YOU UP TO?'

Thrasher took a step backwards. 'I – '

'Don't want to hear it,' Mrs Gobbo said promptly. 'I've never seen you up to any good. And I don't want you in this yard. If I

catch you here again, I'll be round to see your
mother.'

'But I only – '

'OUT!'

Thrasher glared at Barny, Spag and Clipper
as he headed for the gate. Mrs Gobbo
watched him until he was right out of the
yard. Then she pulled her head back inside
and slammed the window.

'I wish *my* mum was terrifying,' Clipper
whispered in Barny's ear. 'No one's scared of
her.'

'Hmmph,' said Barny. He didn't think
Thrasher would be put off that easily. Not if
he really thought there was something valuable in the water tank.

44

'It's a good thing we didn't have to tell him about the FutureScope,' said Spag. 'He'd be sure to tell Soppy Elaine, or someone like that. And we must keep it a secret.'

Clipper nodded. 'It'll spoil the surprises if people know about them beforehand.'

'Suppose so,' Barny said unhappily. He had a nasty feeling that Thrasher's idea about *antiques* was going to cause a lot more trouble.

But for the next few days they didn't see anything of Thrasher at all. Instead, they had to try keeping their secret at school. They managed to avoid talking about projects for a while, but it got harder and harder.

One morning, Spotty McGrew grabbed

Barny as soon as he walked into the classroom.

'Here, Gobbo, what do you think about this? I really got going on my dictionary last night.' He pushed a bundle of paper under Barny's nose.

WHAT WE SHALL BE SAYING IN A HUNDRED YEARS' TIME

it began.

A SLANG DICTIONARY OF THE 21ST CENTURY
by S. McGrew

Then there was a list of words:

McGREW – (as in 'it's a real mcgrew!' or 'My new computer's extra-double mcgrew!) = fabulous, wonderful, the best it can possibly be.

SPAGRAG – (as in 'he's a real spagrag') = a thin, bony person.

GOBBO – (as in 'you've gone absolutely gobbo!') = mad, loony, full of wild ideas.

'Here!' Barny said.

Spotty hooted with laughter and whipped the pages out of Barny's hands before he could do anything to them. 'Brilliant, aren't they? I was killing myself laughing while I was making them up.'

'But you can't – '

'Yes I can. Of course I can.' Spotty chortled wickedly. 'They're absolutely *mcgrew*.'

46

Before Barny could say what he thought about that, Soppy Elaine and Sharon Grove came sweeping into the room with their arms round each other's waists.

'*We're* going to have the best thing of all for Anniversary Day!' announced Elaine, at the top of her voice. 'Guess what my mum's going to do. You'll love it.'

'Send you to Australia?' murmured Clipper.

Elaine was so pleased with herself that she didn't even look annoyed. 'Anyway, you're just jealous, Clipper Young. Because you'll never make your project as good as ours. Me and Sharon aren't just going to have drawings. We're going to have Real Twenty-First-Century Clothes.'

'Made of material,' Sharon said solemnly.

'Copied from our own designs,' said Elaine.

'To *wear*.'

'One outfit each.' Elaine pulled a face at Spotty. 'And guess who's going to win the prize?'

'Me!' said Spotty. He pushed his dictionary under Soppy Elaine's nose. 'Take a look at this.'

She read a few lines and suddenly went bright red. 'You horrible boy! You can't do that! You can't make up words about me!'

But Spotty just grinned. '*Elaining*,' he read out loud, *'(as in 'don't keep elaining on at me!')* = *nagging on in a moaning voice. A mixture of whining and complaining.'*

Elaine shrieked again and marched up the classroom towards Mr Fox, who was just coming through the door with his arms full of books. 'Sir! Sir! You've got to stop Spotty. He's making up *words* about me!'

Mr Fox blinked and dropped half the books. 'Can't you wait a minute, Elaine? Give me a chance to get through the door.'

Spotty grinned. 'She's just jealous, sir. Because I've got on so well with my project.'

Mr Fox put his books down on the desk. 'I'm glad to hear you've been working hard. I just hope other people have been doing the same.' He looked round at Barny, Spag and Clipper. 'It's time you three chose your project.'

'They don't want to bother,' Soppy Elaine

48

said loudly. 'Because they know that mine and Sharon's is sure to be the best.'

'We've got a brilliant project,' snapped Clipper.

'That's right,' said Barny. 'But we can't tell you about it, because it's got to be a secret.'

'A *secret*?' said Mr Fox.

Everyone turned round to look at Barny.

'Be quiet!' hissed Spag.

But Clipper burst in excitedly. 'That's right, sir. It's got to be a secret. If people see it while we're making it, there won't be any surprises.'

'What sort of surprises?' called out Spotty McGrew. 'Free gifts and stuff?'

'*Secret* surprises,' Clipper said.

Spag groaned and buried his head in his hands.

Mr Fox raised his eyebrows. 'Not *too* secret, I hope. You're supposed to be working on your projects this morning. I can't give you a room of your own.'

'That's OK, sir.' Clipper waved at the craft corner. 'I'll make a few models.'

'And I need to go to the library,' said Spag. 'To look up figures and check facts and copy diagrams.'

Mr Fox beamed. 'And what about you, Gobbo?'

'I – er – '

'Why don't you make the notices?' Clipper said helpfully. 'To go over the pipes. You only need to write the words on card. And think of a way to make hinges and – '

'Sssshhh!' said Barny and Spag, both together.

But it was too late. Everyone began to ask questions.

'Is it a jack-in-the-box – ?'

' – something to do with drains?'

' – musical instruments?'

Mr Fox banged on the table. 'Leave these three alone and get on with your own projects.'

Grumbling and mumbling, people went off to work.

'Don't forget!' Spag hissed at Barny and Clipper. 'Keep it *secret*.'

Barny got some sheets of white card and

sat down to make notices. But he had only cut out two, rather wobbly, squares of card when Soppy Elaine passed him a note.

What's Clipper doing? it said.

Barny looked across at the craft corner. Clipper's fingers were flashing. She had made a tiny, delicate windmill, out of wood and cardboard, and she was just starting on another.

Don't know Barny scrawled across the bottom of the note. Then he flicked it back to Elaine. She read it, stuck out her tongue and turned her back on him.

With a sigh of relief, Barny went on with his notices. But not for long. A few moments later, Spotty McGrew came past, with a pile of dictionaries.

'What's the matter with Spag?' he hissed. 'He's sitting in the library moaning because there aren't enough books.'

'Spag doesn't moan,' Barny said.

'You should hear him!' Spotty pulled a face. 'He wants books on electricity and the oceans and food and – '

Mr Fox came up behind Spotty and laid a heavy hand on his shoulder. 'Problems? Getting help from Gobbo, are you?'

'Of course not!' Spotty said furiously.

'Go and get on with your work then. Two pages don't make a dictionary, you know. However good they are.'

'They're *mcgrew*!' muttered Spotty. But he went away.

Barny looked down at his notices. Some of the corners had got bent and there was a big thumbprint in the middle of one. He decided to stop cutting out squares and do some writing. Picking up a felt pen, he began on the first notice, in big, black letters.

HOW WILL WE GET OUR ELECTR

But before he could get any further, he found Sharon Grove breathing down his neck. Angrily, he put his hand over the card.

'Stop spying!'

'Oh, go on!' Sharon gave him a sugary smile. 'Let me see. I won't tell anyone else. Promise.'

'Oh yes you will!' Barny put his other hand on top of the first one. 'You'll tell Elaine. And she'll tell everyone in the world.'

'Don't be so *mean*!'

Sharon's bottom lip trembled and her eyes began to fill with tears.

'Go away!' Barny hissed.

'But I only – '

'Go *away*!'

Mr Fox looked across at them. 'What's the matter *now*, Gobbo?'

Sharon shot away, across the room, and Barny went on trying to work. But he had smudged his writing when he covered it up, so he had to begin all over again.

It went on like that, all the morning. Every two or three minutes, someone leaned over his shoulder, asking awkward questions.

And it was just the same for Spag and Clipper.

'It's *hopeless*!' growled Spag when they met at lunch time. 'There's no peace here. I'll have to take all the books home to read them.'

Clipper nodded. 'I've only made six windmills. And the tree for the criminals to chop down. I had people snooping round me *all the time*.'

'We'll have to do it at home,' Barny said. 'If we work every evening, we should get it all done.'

'It's still going to be hard to keep it secret,' Spag said gloomily.

He was right. The questions went on all day. And at the end of school people clustered round them in the cloakroom.

'You going to bring your project to school tomorrow?' said Spotty.

Barny shook his head. 'Not till Anniversary Day,' said Barny.

'You *see*?' said Soppy Elaine. 'They haven't got anything really. It's all pretend.'

'It is *not* pretend!' Barny said furiously. 'We've got lots of stuff. But we're keeping it all at my house until Anniversary Day.'

Spag nudged him and frowned. 'Sshh!'

But it was too late. Everyone in the cloak-room had heard what Barny said. And a huge grin was spreading across Spotty's face.

'I think we ought to go and take a look at this project of theirs,' he said loudly. 'Don't you?'

The answers came from all around.

'Yeah!'

'Great!'

'Let's follow them.'

'You and your big mouth!' Clipper hissed at Barny.

'Let's try and beat them,' muttered Spag. 'Come on! Run!'

He shot out of the cloakroom, with Clipper close behind. Barny blinked.

'Here! Wait for – '

But they'd gone. Grabbing his bag, he raced out of the cloakroom after them. But it was no use. Clipper could run twice as fast as he could. By the time he reached the school gates, she and Spag were out of sight round the corner.

But he wasn't alone. The rest of the class were all round him, pushing and shoving and giggling as they followed him home.

He hadn't the faintest idea how to get rid of them.

4

Snoopers

By the time they reached the scrapyard, Barny was almost last. The others didn't wait for him. They pushed their way in through the gates and spread out all over the yard.

'Come on, everyone!' shouted Spotty. 'Let's

find it. I bet he's got it hidden in the yard. That's where Gobbo keeps all his secrets.'

'Stop!' Barny said. 'Come out! This is private property.'

Soppy Elaine and Sharon looked rather nervous, but the others just laughed and began peering behind piles of chairs, and into enormous flowerpots. Most of them stayed near the gate, but Spotty McGrew headed off across the yard, towards the far corner.

Barny watched him getting nearer and nearer to the water tank. All Clipper's models and Spag's notes were stored inside it. If Spotty found those . . .

Barny wished that his mother would suddenly appear and sort them all out. But Thursday was her afternoon for visiting his grandmother, and she wouldn't be home for an hour.

People kept asking loud, excited questions.

'Is your stuff in the house?'

'Has it got anything to do with this old television?'

'Are your mum and dad helping you with it?'

Clipper and Spag were nowhere to be seen. Feeling rather dazed, Barny stood in the gateway looking for them.

'Gobbo won't tell you anything,' Spotty called. 'We've got to *search*.' And he squeezed his way through to the fireplaces beside the water tank.

People turned their backs on Barny and began to wander off. He was just about to give up and wait for them to find the tank when a voice hissed loudly, from beside his feet.

'Psst! Gobbo!'

It was Spag's voice. And it was coming from a big pipe, behind a pile of sinks. Several other people heard it, besides Barny, and they turned round to look.

'Sssh!' whispered Barny.

But Spag didn't take any notice. 'Have they gone?' he hissed, even louder.

'No they haven't,' muttered Barny.

'Fantastic,' hissed Clipper, in an even louder whisper. 'It's working brilliantly, isn't it?'

Barny hadn't got a clue what she was talking about. Working? What was working? Spotty was just about to discover their project, and ruin everything.

'They haven't guessed it's a trick, have they?' said Spag's voice.

It echoed in the hollow pipe, and people began to crowd round to listen. From the far side of the yard, Spotty saw them, just as he reached the water tank.

'Here!' he called. 'What's going on?'

No one answered, because they were keeping quiet, to listen to Spag and Clipper. But one or two people beckoned. Spotty turned

and begin to pick his way back, past the
fireplaces and round the tiles.

'They really think our project is here?'
Clipper's voice said, loud and clear.

Suddenly Barny realised what was going

on. He thumped the side of the pipe and pretended to look horrified.

'Quiet!' he hissed.

'Yes, get your voice down, Clipper.' Spag spoke more softly, but not too softly to be heard outside. 'We don't want them guessing the stuff's at your house.'

'Oh you dumbos!' Barny pulled a terrible face and covered his eyes with his hands.

Immediately, Elaine let out a yelp of triumph. 'We heard that, Clipper Young! And we're going to find your stupid project. *If* you've got one.'

Spag and Clipper gasped with horror inside the pipe, but hardly anyone heard them. Running feet clattered across the yard, with lots of clanging and rattling as people bumped into things. Then the gate fell shut, with a great wooden thud, and there was silence.

Barny waited for Spag and Clipper to crawl out of the pipe, but no one appeared. After a moment or two, he bent down and looked in, to see what had happened to them.

They were curled up with laughter, rolling from side to side with their hands over their mouths to keep the sound in.

'It's OK,' Barny said. 'You can come out now.'

Clipper crawled out on all fours, gasping for breath. 'The best thing – ' she panted, as soon as she could speak ' – is – everyone's out

– at my house. They won't be able to find out – that they're wrong – and so – '

'And so the project will be safe!' Spag said triumphantly. 'No one will look for it *here*. Wasn't my idea brilliant?'

'Fabulous,' said Clipper. 'But we haven't got time to stand round admiring you. We've got to *make* the thing now. Come on.' She began to hustle them towards the water tank. 'I want to start putting models into the plastic bottles. We can do the wind park now. And the ocean full of pingpong balls. The tree-cutting criminals are almost ready too.'

They spent the rest of the afternoon working on the FutureScope. By evening, three of the bottles were finished, with their models set up and fixed inside. Clipper laid them carefully down at the back of the water tank and looked at them with a grin.

'It's going to be absolutely – absolutely *mcgrew!!!*'

'Yes,' said Spag. 'We'll amaze everybody on Anniversary Day. Have you fixed up with your dad yet, Gobbo? About his lorry?'

'I – er – ' Barny shuffled his feet. He wasn't sure his dad would understand about the FutureScope. Not unless he could see it all, completely finished. 'I'll ask him soon.'

'Well, don't hang about,' Clipper said. 'We'll look pretty stupid if we can't get it there, after all this work.'

'I *told* you. I'll ask him in the next day or so.'

But it wasn't that simple. For the next week or so, Barny hardly saw his dad at all. Mr Gobbo was busy driving round the country, collecting lorry-loads of scrap, so he left very early and got home late. And Barny was even busier.

He had never guessed that the FutureScope would make so much work. There were models to be planned ('. . . yes, but how are we going to make the school *look* flooded? . . . of course we can't fill the bottle with water!'), models to be fixed ('. . . just hold it in the tweezers, Gobbo, and drop it into place . . . no, you dimbo, on the GLUE!') and models to be kept secret.

Keeping the secret from Spotty was the hardest thing. The other people in the class lost interest, but Spotty didn't. He was determined to find out what they were up to. Two or three times a week he sneaked after them when they left school.

But he wasn't very good at shadowing.

'Spies!' Clipper would whisper. 'Look behind that lamppost.'

When that happened, they pretended not to notice Spotty. But they headed for Clipper's house, instead of the scrapyard. It had a solid front door, and the three of them shut it firmly in Spotty's face.

He got angrier and angrier and lots of new words appeared in his dictionary. Words like *barnism* ('keeping stupid secrets') and *clipperage* ('banging doors dangerously close to people's noses'). But he didn't give up.

And then they came out of school one afternoon and found Thrasher leaning against the wall. And he wasn't alone. Tiny Dyson was beside him, looking tall and wide and very, very solid.

When Barny, Spag and Clipper appeared, a large, nasty grin spread across Tiny Dyson's face.

'Well, well, well, we were just talking about you. I hear you've struck it rich.'

'Struck it – what?' Barny blinked.

'Don't try to fool me,' said Tiny Dyson. 'You've found something valuable in that yard of yours, haven't you? Something my Uncle Des would be *really* interested in.'

'Your Uncle – ?' began Barny.

Spag nudged him. 'He's talking about antiques, Gobbo. Remember what Thrasher said, when we caught him playing tortoises with that tin bath?'

Thrasher clenched his fists. 'Nearly got you then, didn't I? Another minute and I'd have been close enough to hear what you were up to.'

'But there's nothing to hear,' Clipper said. 'Nothing that would interest you, anyway.'

'Don't give us that.' Tiny Dyson bent down until his huge face was level with Clipper's. 'We *know*, see? You gave the game away when you told Thresher you'd got something *valuable*. And we want to be in on it.'

'But there's nothing to be in on,' Barny said desperately. 'It's all a – a misunderstanding.'

Tiny Dyson smirked. 'You must think we're really daft if you expect us to believe that. Eh, Thrash?'

'Yeah,' jeered Thrasher. 'If you haven't got antiques in that tank of yours – why is it such a secret? Why won't you tell us what's going on?'

'We *will* tell you,' Barny said quickly. 'We don't have to keep it secret from you. We were just – '

But before he could get any further, Clipper nudged him. 'Spies!' she hissed.

Spotty had just come out of school and was strolling towards them.

'We – we – 'stuttered Barny.

'Come on,' Tiny Dyson said. 'We're waiting, Gobbo. What's your secret?'

He spoke so loudly that Spotty heard him and broke into a run, to get closer. Barny didn't know what to do. If he explained now, Spotty would hear what he said and their secret would be finished. But if he didn't explain . . .

'Come on, Gobbo,' said Thrasher. 'Tell us what you're doing.'

'I – '

There was only one way out.

'RUN!' said Barny.

The three of them raced off up the road. Thrasher and Tiny didn't bother to follow, but Barny could hear them laughing, even when he was round the corner.

There was going to be trouble. He knew there was.

It was very hot that night. So hot that Mrs Gobbo came in and opened Barny's bedroom window on her way to bed. But, even with the window open, Barny was so hot that he tossed and turned and kept waking up.

The first three times, he only woke for a second or two. Just long enough to sit up and let the air cool him down. Then his head hit the pillow and he was asleep again.

But the fourth time was different.

Just after midnight, when Mr and Mrs Gobbo were fast asleep across the landing, he found himself suddenly awake. It wasn't the heat this time. Something else had woken him.

His bedroom was the only one that looked over the scrapyard. And through his window, from down in the scrapyard, came queer shuffling, scraping noises.

For a few moments he lay staring at the ceiling, trying to work out what was going on.

Cats? Too clumsy.

People going along the street? No. They sounded closer than that. And they didn't move away.

Burglars?

Barny froze for a moment, lying like a statue under the covers. It really might be burglars! What could he do?

If he called out to his parents, the burglars would hear him. If he got up to look through the window, they might see him. But he

65

couldn't just keep quiet and let them burgle the yard. *What was he going to do?*

For a few more seconds he lay there, with his heart thudding. If only the noises would go away! But they didn't. They changed. The scraping stopped and he could hear strange footsteps outside. They sounded slow and creaky, but he couldn't work out what was going on. If only he could see . . .

Very, very slowly and carefully, he rolled out of bed on to the mat and crawled across the floor. When he was beside the window he straightened up, with his back to the wall. Keeping his body hidden behind the curtain, he peered cautiously round the window frame.

There was a ladder outside the yard, leaning up against the wall. He could see the top of it sticking up above the bricks. The scraping must have been the sound of the ladder being put into place.

As he watched, a dark shape appeared, climbing up the ladder. It threw one leg over the wall and sat on top. Then, slowly and rather noisily, it pulled up the ladder and let it down on the other side. Inside the yard.

Barny's heart thudded even faster. It *was* burglars! He had to tell his mum and dad. But could he do that, without being seen or heard?

While he was hesitating, the dark figure climbed down the ladder into the yard. It

wasn't a very *big* burglar, Barny thought.
Not much bigger than him. But what was it
after?

The burglar pulled out a torch and shone it
carefully round the yard. The narrow beam
of light flickered over the stack of old tiles,
past three fireplaces, and round the pile of
basins.

Whatever the dark figure had come to steal, it
wasn't any of those. The light flitted on impatiently, moving from one thing to another.

Then it hit the FutureScope.

At once, the movement stopped. For a
moment the burglar held the torch steady,
shining the light straight at the water tank.

Barny stopped thinking about calling his
parents. He kept very still and watched to see
what would happen. Silently, the dark figure
started to move across the yard. It picked its
way past the tiles. It squeezed round the
basins, holding them steady with one hand.
And then it tiptoed behind the fireplaces.

There was no doubt about it. It was head-
ing for the FutureScope.

Barny forgot about being frightened and
began to be angry instead. The burglar was
already bending down, to crawl inside the
water tank. In another moment, he would be
looking into the bottles. And then the secret
would be spoilt.

Leaning out of his window, Barny yelled

67

at the top of his voice. 'WHO ARE YOU?
WHAT ARE YOU DOING IN OUR
YARD?'

The figure straightened suddenly, and there
was a gigantic clang as its head hit the top

of the water tank. Then it staggered out,
weaving dizzily, with its torch waving everywhere.

'GO AWAY!' yelled Barny. 'I'M CALLING
THE POLICE!'

Charging for the gate, the burglar cannoned into the basins. They toppled over and fell sideways. One of them hit the water tank with a crash, breaking into dozens of jagged pieces.

Across the landing, Barny heard his father wake up. His feet thudded on to the floor and he yelled over his shoulder to Mrs Gobbo as he raced for the stairs.

'Phone the police! There's burglars in the yard!'

The burglar must have heard the shout too. He leaped frantically away from the tank, stumbling against the fireplaces as he went.

Six fireplaces slid to the ground with a clang and next to them a pile of tiles overbalanced. Slowly, one by one, they started to slither to the ground and smash.

With a roar of rage, Mr Gobbo threw open the front door and began to charge across the yard.

The burglar raced for the ladder. By the time Mr Gobbo was halfway across the yard, the dark figure had reached the top of the wall. He didn't bother to shift the ladder. Desperately, he threw his legs over the wall, the lighted torch still clutched in one hand, its beam swinging wildly.

For a split second, the torchlight flitted across a wild, desperate face. It was a face that Barny knew very well indeed.

The face of Thrasher Dyson.

Barny gasped, but he was too amazed to do anything. And a split second later, Thrasher was over the wall, dropping down on to the pavement.

The next moment, Barny heard him running away up the street. Mr Gobbo climbed the ladder and stared after the running feet, but he was much too late to catch them. After a moment or two, he climbed down again and carried the ladder away to the far side of the yard.

Slowly, Barny padded back to bed, wondering what to do next.

'It was really him again?' Spag said, the next morning. 'The Great Thrasher Dyson? Are you sure?'

'Course I'm sure. Think I'm blind?'

'But why on earth – ?'

'You know why,' said Clipper. 'Because he thinks we've got *antiques* in the water tank.'

Spag shook his head. 'He can't be serious about that.'

'He is,' said Clipper. 'Or he wouldn't have told Tiny. Honestly, Gobbo, you were *dumb* to start teasing him about how *valuable* our project was.'

'*Me?*' Barny spluttered. '*I* didn't start it. It was you and Spag – '

'Oh no it wasn't. You were the one who – '

71

Spag put his hands over his ears. 'Doesn't matter whose fault it was, does it? The point is – we're stuck with Thrasher snooping around. What are we going to do?'

'Think we should tell the police who Gobbo's burglar was?' said Clipper.

Barny remembered how desperate Thrasher had looked when he was climbing over the wall. 'No point, is there? Dad didn't actually lose anything. I don't think the police were really interested.'

Spag frowned. 'Aren't they worried he might come back?'

Barny grinned. 'They told my dad he ought to have a burglar alarm. But he said he wasn't having one of those going off all the time. Said he'd rather trust his own ears.'

Clipper spluttered with laughter, but Spag looked thoughtful.

'A burglar alarm's not a bad idea,' he said slowly. 'We could have one to protect the FutureScope. It wouldn't be very difficult to make.'

He pulled out his notebook and wandered off, scribbling busily.

5

The Burglar Maze

For the rest of the day, Spag hardly spoke to
Barny and Clipper. Every time he had a spare
moment, he was busy with his notebook,
drawing little diagrams and muttering to
himself.

But as soon as school finished, he grabbed

them. 'I've got it!' he said triumphantly, waving his notebook. 'I've worked out the most brilliant – '

'Ssh!' said Barny. Soppy Elaine and Sharon were just coming into the cloakroom. He didn't want *them* hearing anything.

'Let's go to the – to where we're working,' Clipper said quickly. 'Come on. Race you there!'

Spag was so eager that he almost kept up with her. The moment they were all inside the FutureScope he pulled out his drawings and spread them over everyone's knees.

'It's a very simple plan,' he said excitedly. 'It's all based on black thread. The kind for sewing on buttons.'

'Thread?' Barny looked scornful. 'You can't catch Thrasher with *thread*. It's not nearly strong enough.'

'It's not meant to catch him,' Spag said impatiently. 'It's meant to give a warning. Look.'

He flapped his diagrams under Barny's nose. 'We wind it round the things in the yard – like this – and this – and this and he'll never notice it.'

Barny frowned. 'But – '

'*Listen!*' said Spag. 'When he gets tangled up, he'll pull the thread. And that will bring something crashing to the ground.'

Clipper nodded slowly. 'That'll tell us if

he's snooping around. But what about us? We'll never get to the FutureScope if it's all wound up in black cotton.'

Spag looked very pleased with himself. 'That's what makes this such a brilliant burglar alarm. There's a way through. Like in a maze.'

He held out one of the drawings and began to trace a path slowly through the tangled lines, between blobs that said things like *fireplaces* and *basins*.

'See? There's a gap here and here and here. If you know how to zigzag, from one gap to another, you can get through. But anyone who doesn't know will get caught up in the thread.'

Clipper looked doubtful. 'Sounds very fiddly. You do it if you want to. I'm going to look at the models. I bet Thrasher knocked something over when he was crashing about last night.'

She crouched over the plastic bottles, and groaned when she found a broken windmill. But the damage wasn't too bad and, in a few seconds, she was busy fixing things.

'Come on, Gobbo.' Spag pulled Barny outside. 'Let's get going on the burglar alarm. Do you think your mother will give us some black thread?'

'Go and ask her,' Barny said. 'I'll look round the yard. We need some things that'll make a noise if they're pulled over.'

'Make sure they're things your dad won't want,' said Spag. 'We don't want to annoy him.'

Barny nodded and wandered off. The yard was a fabulous place to hunt for junk. Things were stacked under and over and inside other things, in towering, tottering piles. Some of the objects were so peculiar that Barney couldn't guess what they were for.

There were plenty of things that would make a noise. He found three old brass bells, a heap of six tin trays and a set of blackened billycans. Carrying everything on the biggest tray, he began to pick his way back across the yard to the FutureScope.

Spag had already started winding thread round the piles of junk. When he saw Barny coming, he jumped up and waved his arms. 'Wait! You can't just walk through. You'll get caught.'

'What am I supposed to do?' Barny said crossly. 'I can't hold this lot much longer, you know.'

'Do what I say.' Spag began to shout instructions. 'Not that way! You'll get tangled. Go to the left. No, the left, you dumbo! That's right. NO! LEFT!'

Barny wavered right, then left, then right again. His foot caught in a thread, he swerved to untangle himself – and suddenly his legs were wrapped in black cotton. He wobbled, lost his balance and went crashing to the ground. Trays and bells and billycans landed all around him with a deafening clatter.

The window opened and Mrs Gobbo's head shot out. 'Barny Gobbo! What's going on?'

Barny lifted his head out of a basket. 'Nothing, Mum. Honest. We're just working on our project for Anniversary Day.'

'Hmmph,' said Mrs Gobbo. 'Projects weren't that noisy when *I* was at school.'

But she pulled her head in and shut the window again.

Spag looked down at Barny with a pleased grin. 'You see? The burglar alarm really does work!'

Barny rubbed his bottom. 'It'll catch burglars all right. But how are *we* ever going to get through?'

'You'll learn,' Spag said airily. He stepped neatly round the tangled thread and began picking up the things Barny had dropped.

Suddenly he stopped, with a tray under his arm and a handful of billycans. A big grin spread over his face. 'Hey, look! Shall we use this too? It would make a lovely crash.'

He reached down into a forgotten corner, between two heaps of chairs, and pulled up a vase. It was huge – over half a metre tall – and shaped like a fat mermaid, with a greenish face.

Clipper stuck her head out of the water tank to see what he had found. 'Yuck! She looks seasick. And she's even fatter than Gobbo.'

'She'll make a lovely booby trap.' Spag placed the mermaid lovingly on top of a rickety chest of drawers and tied some black thread round her tail. 'If she falls off, she won't just make a noise. She'll probably knock the burglar out as well.'

Clipper pulled a face at the mermaid and grabbed Barny's arm. 'Come on, Gobbo. Leave that to Spag. I need you to help me with the twenty-first-century pop group.'

'I thought you'd done that,' Barny said. 'Didn't you make those models at school today?'

'Oh, I've done the models,' said Clipper. 'But we're going to have a cassette that plays when you lift the flap. Remember? So we've got to make up a song.'

'A *song?*' Barny swallowed. 'But I can't sing.'

'Yes you can,' Clipper said briskly. 'Don't be so feeble, Gobbo. We're going to make up something really *weird*.'

'It's sure to be weird if Gobbo's singing,' muttered Spag.

'My singing's not weird!' Barny looked furious. 'My grandma says I've got a lovely voice – '

'Just what I've been telling you!' crowed Clipper. 'Come on.' She dragged Barny into the water tank and pushed him into one corner. 'Let's get started.'

Taking her mouth organ out of her pocket, she began to play a strange, jigging tune, banging out the rhythm with her foot, against the side of the tank. After a second or two, she stopped playing, just long enough to say, 'Groan!'

'What?'

'*Groan!*'

'Ugh!' Barny groaned.

'Brilliant!' said Clipper. She played a few more notes and then stopped again. 'Two groans.'

'Ugh! Ugh!'

Clipper grinned, went on playing and nodded to show when she wanted him to groan again. After a minute or two they were into the swing of it, playing and tapping and groaning as loudly as they could. Then Spag crawled into the tank with his hands over his ears.

'Stop! Stop! It's *dreadful!*'

Clipper chuckled. 'That's just what you'll be saying about pop songs in a hundred years' time. Let's go to your house and tape it.'

Spag pulled a face, but he nodded. Crawling out of the tank again, he stood and waited for the other two.

'Follow me!' he hissed as they came out of
the tank. 'And MIND YOU DON'T MAKE
A MISTAKE!'

Carefully, he began to zigzag through the
black cotton maze. Clipper followed, and
Barny came last, trying hard to do exactly the
same as Spag.

They brushed the threads a few times, and
once the fat green mermaid tottered dangerously, while the three of them held their
breath. But they got through the burglar
alarm without any disasters.

Clipper looked back at it. 'Hmm. Not bad.
You can play my mouth organ if you like.
On the tape.'

Spag shook his head. 'No thanks. I'll never

manage to make such a horrible noise as you do.'

Clipper growled and chased him all the way home, with Barny panting along behind.

They spent nearly an hour recording the groan song. In the end, Spag's mother threw them out because she couldn't stand it any longer. They had got quite fond of it by then, and as they walked back to the scrapyard they all sang it together, humming and groaning and tapping their feet on the pavement.

'This is a star project,' Clipper said, as they came round the corner. 'We've got the best idea, we've almost finished making it, *and* we've written a song.'

'Ugh!' said Barny.

'Ugh! Ugh!' said Spag.

Clipper was just going to groan back, when a loud voice came floating over the wall of the scrapyard.

'Good evening, Mrs Gobbo. I just happened to glance in at the gate as I passed, and I saw that delightful piece over there. Would it be possible to look more closely?'

Barny's eyes opened wide and he looked at Spag and Clipper. They knew that voice. Only too well.

Then another voice joined in. And they knew that one even better.

'Oh *do* buy it, Mummy. It's such a dear

little mermaid. I love its green face. It's sweet! Please, please – '

'It's not *sweet*, Elaine,' said the first voice. 'It's a very fine piece of china. Probably valuable. Stay here while I have a closer look.'

'Oh no!' Clipper whispered. She and Barny and Spag crept to the gate and peered round it into the yard, hoping they had heard wrong.

But they hadn't. There in the yard were Soppy Elaine and her mother. Elaine was standing by the house, gazing at the mermaid vase. There was a sickly grin on her face and her hands were clasped under her chin.

Soppy Mrs Potter was striding across the yard towards the vase. Another three steps and she would reach the black thread. It might have been better to sneak quietly away, but Barny didn't think of that in time. He leaped forward and shouted. 'Mrs Potter! Stop!'

Mrs Potter turned round and raised her eyebrows. 'I beg your pardon?'

'Please, Mrs Potter, don't go and get that vase. It's – it's – '

'It's no use,' Clipper said over his shoulder. 'It leaks.'

'And it's not painted very well,' said Spag.

'And it's *not* valuable,' said Barny. 'Honestly it isn't.'

'It's hard for children to appreciate true art,'

82

Mrs Potter said graciously. 'For *some* children, at least.' She smiled proudly at Elaine, over her shoulder. 'I'm almost certain that that is a valuable piece of Staffordshire china.'

'B–but you don't understand – ' Barny spluttered.

'Who doesn't understand?' said a loud voice. Mrs Gobbo looked suddenly through the window. 'We'll have a bit more politeness from you, Barny Gobbo.' She nodded at Mrs Potter. 'Take a look if you want. I'm coming out.'

'But, *Mum* – '

Mrs Gobbo glared at Barny until he was silent, and then disappeared from the kitchen window. Mrs Potter turned back to the mermaid vase. She took two more steps.

'Please!' said Barny.

'You leave Mummy alone,' said Elaine. 'You're really rude, Gobbo.'

Mrs Potter glanced over her shoulder. 'Elaine! His name is Barny. Not *Gobbo*.'

She took a third step, still looking backwards, and suddenly her face changed. Her mouth opened wide and her eyebrows went up.

'I've caught my foot – '

'Keep still!' said Clipper.

But Mrs Potter ignored her. She took another step – and suddenly the scrapyard seemed to come to life around her. A stack of trays tipped up and clattered to the ground. Six billycans tumbled on to her head from the top of a wardrobe. Bells flew everywhere, ringing wildly as they knocked off her hat and tipped her sideways. She sat down with a bump, right in the middle of the thickest patch of black cotton.

And then, very slowly and gracefully, the fat green mermaid tipped forward. It tumbled off a stack of tables, bouncing on each one. The fishy tail cracked and flew off in one direction. The arms snapped and fell off on the other side. And the main part of the vase landed, upside down, on Mrs Potter's head.

For a moment there was a terrible, horrified silence. Then Soppy Elaine wailed at the top of her voice.

'The mermaid's *broken!*'

'Never mind the mermaid!' snapped Mrs Potter, pushing the broken vase off her head. 'What about *me?* I can't move. My feet are tied together.'

'Oh – um – ' Spag ran his fingers through his hair until it stood on end. 'I'm really sorry, Mrs Potter. We didn't mean – that is, it wasn't for you – '

Mrs Gobbo appeared in the doorway. She took one look at Mrs Potter and bellowed at Barny.

'Scissors! Now!'

Barny raced for the big kitchen scissors and in a few seconds Mrs Gobbo was marching across the yard.

Mrs Potter eyed the scissors nervously. 'I hope you'll be careful with those.'

'Just keep still,' grunted Mrs Gobbo.

She bent over and began to snip. It took her two or three minutes to get rid of all the black thread, but at last she straightened and stepped back. 'There you are. No harm done.'

Mrs Potter sniffed. 'Oh yes there is! Look at the state of my clothes. They'll have to be drycleaned straight away. And I shall need new tights as well.' She levered herself off the ground. 'I shall expect you to pay for all that, Mrs Gobbo.'

Barny went red in the face. 'That's not fair!'

'We told you not to go over there,' said Clipper.

Mrs Gobbo gave Mrs Potter a small, tight-lipped smile. 'Of course I'll pay your bills. But you'll have to settle up with me. For the breakages.'

'The breakages?' Mrs Potter went white. 'What do you mean?'

Mrs Gobbo pointed at the remains of the mermaid vase. 'That's a valuable piece of china. You said it yourself.'

'I – I didn't mean,' stuttered Mrs Potter. 'That is – shall we forget the whole matter?'

Mrs Gobbo stared thoughtfully at her for a moment. Then she gave a slow, heavy nod, without smiling. Immediately, Mrs Potter grabbed Elaine's hand and headed for the gate.

The moment they were out of sight, Barny, Spag and Clipper started to laugh, leaning against each other and gasping for breath.

'Honestly, Mrs Gobbo,' panted Clipper, 'you were brilliant!'

'You really told her, Mum,' said Barny.

Spag nodded. 'Her face! When she realised she'd broken that vase! Was it really valuable?'

'Dad won it at the fair,' Mrs Gobbo said. 'On the hoopla stall.'

Barny, Spag and Clipper fell about again, laughing so much that their sides ached.

But Mrs Gobbo wasn't smiling. She stood there with her arms folded until the three of them stopped laughing.

Barny gulped down his last giggle. 'What's the matter, Mum?'

'You're the matter!' Mrs Gobbo said grimly. 'What's been going on out here?'

'It was – ' Barny began.

But Mrs Gobbo wasn't interested in his explanations. 'We can't afford to have customers breaking their legs.'

'It was an accident, Mum,' Barny said quickly. He could tell from her face that something nasty was going to happen. But he didn't guess how nasty.

'This is a scrapyard, not a playground,' she said. 'And we can't afford this sort of carry-on. You'll have to find somewhere else for your games.'

'Somewhere else?' squeaked Barny.

Clipper's mouth fell open. 'You mean – we can't play in the scrapyard any more?'

'That's right,' said Mrs Gobbo. 'Clear up all that thread and then take yourselves off. You're welcome to come into the house, but I don't want to see you out here any more.'

Barny looked across at the FutureScope and then back at his mother. 'But, Mum – '

'*No*,' said Mrs Gobbo.

6

Banished

'What are we going to *do?*' Clipper said desperately. 'Can't you *explain* to your mother, Gobbo?'

Barny stared gloomily out at her back garden. 'I could explain all right. But it wouldn't make any difference. She never changes her mind about things like that.'

'But Anniversary Day is next week,' Spag said. 'And we won't have a project at all.'

'It's infuriating!' Clipper was almost exploding. 'We've *got* to go back and ask your mum, Gobbo.'

'No! That'll ruin everything!'

Spag frowned. 'So what *are* we going to do?'

'Well – ' Barny said slowly, 'we could do most of the work at your house. We'd only need an hour or two in the yard, wouldn't we? When everything was ready.'

'So what?' said Clipper. 'Two hours or two weeks – what's the difference? If we can't come into the yard, we can't come in at all.'

'Well – ' Barny said, even more slowly, 'Anniversary Day isn't until next Wednesday. And on Tuesday evenings my mum and dad go out to play darts.'

'So?' said Clipper.

'So my nan comes in to look after me.'

Suddenly Clipper and Spag looked hopeful.

'You mean – '

'Do you think we could – ?'

Barny nodded. 'We've got almost a week to make the rest of the models. On Tuesday evening we'll sneak them over there. We can put the FutureScope together and paint the outside while Nan's asleep in front of the TV. She'd sleep through a brass band concert.'

'Brilliant!' said Clipper.

But Spag didn't look so sure. 'There's not much point in finishing it unless we can get it to school. And if your parents are angry because we've been in the yard, your dad won't take it on his lorry, will he?'

'He might,' Barny said. 'When he sees how fantastic it is. Mum might persuade him. She really wants us to win that prize, instead of Elaine.'

'It'll be OK,' Clipper said firmly. 'It's got to be. It's our only chance.'

It was a breathless week. Spag spent the whole time drawing diagrams.

'We need a foolproof way of fixing the bottles on,' he kept muttering. 'And some kind of switch. So the cassette player comes on when the pop group flap is lifted. And a curtain for the front –'

Every time he moved, diagrams fluttered out of his pockets. Spotty McGrew nearly went mad trying to work out what they were.

'Come on, Spag. Give us a clue. Is it a model building you're making? Or a game where the answer lights up? Just say yes or no. Don't be so – *spagnoid*.'

Clipper was busy, too. She still had dozens of models to make, and every time she went to the craft corner Elaine fluttered up.

'You're not making *more* little people? Honestly, I don't know why you're bothering. You haven't got a hope of winning the prize. Sharon and me are going to have the best project in The Exhibition. The Public will love it.'

Elaine had a special smile that she used when she talked about The Public and The Exhibition. Spotty called it a pottersmirk. There were lots of Soppy Elaine words in his dictionary now. It was already seventy-two pages long.

'And it'll be a hundred pages by Exhibition Day,' Spotty kept saying. 'You wait and see. The Public's really going to enjoy reading it.'

Elaine sniffed and swept off and Clipper heaved a sigh of relief. She hadn't got time to waste on Elaine. She was making tiny little pandas and tigers, out of scraps of furry material, and it was more difficult than she had expected . . .

They thought they were never going to finish in time, but somehow they did. By the end of Tuesday afternoon, everything was done. They slid the last of the models into carrier bags and hurried home.

'See you at eight o'clock,' hissed Clipper, as they parted outside Barny's house.

'Don't forget to unlock the gate,' whispered Spag.

Barny nodded and pushed them off down the road. He didn't want his mother to over-hear anything. She had a very suspicious mind.

It was difficult to go on looking innocent all through tea-time. Barny tried as hard as he could, but his mother kept feeling his forehead.

'You sure you're all right? Not sickening for anything?'

'Of course I'm not.'

'I don't know. Perhaps I shouldn't go tonight – '

'I'm fine, Mum. Honest I am.' Desperately Barny searched for a way to convince her. 'I'm just tired. We've been doing a lot of work for Anniversary Day.'

'Hmmph.' Mrs Gobbo picked up her coat, but she was still watching Barny. 'Well, you'd better go to bed early. Don't wait for Nan to send you.'

'Yes I will. No I won't. Bye, Mum.'

Mrs Gobbo put an arm into the coat. 'Bit keen to get rid of me, aren't you? You plotting something?'

'Course not!' Barny opened his eyes wide. 'I just thought you were ready.'

'Hmm.'

Mrs Gobbo frowned. But Barny went on looking as innocent as he could and at last she went, calling instructions to his grandmother over her shoulder.

'Now don't let him bother you, Mum.
And mind he goes to bed quite soon.'

Barny's nan smiled and waved and nodded.
And the moment Mr and Mrs Gobbo had
gone, she switched the television on and sat
down in front of it.

'Be a good boy now,' she muttered. 'And
remember I can hear everything you do.'

Barny grinned and looked at the kitchen
clock. Fifteen minutes. That was all it usually
took Nan to fall asleep once she sat down. He
gave her twenty minutes, to be on the safe
side, and then peeped into the living room.
Sure enough, she was snoring away, with the
television going full blast.

Very carefully, Barny pulled the living-
room door shut. Then he tiptoed across the

94

hall and took the yard key off the hook by the front door.

For a moment he thought that Clipper and Spag were already waiting for him. He could see two pairs of feet, under the bottom of the gate. And as he walked across the yard he heard the voices whispering outside.

But when he unlocked the gate and flung it open, there was no one there. Only two dark figures hurrying away towards the corner of the road. Surely that wasn't them?

'Clipper?' Barny called softly. 'Spag?'

The black figures didn't turn round. Instead, a voice shouted from the other direction.

'Cooee! Gobbo!'

Clipper and Spag were coming up the road towards him. Clipper was pushing a loaded wheelbarrow and Spag was carrying two bulging plastic bags.

'Cooee!' Clipper shouted again, waving one hand. The wheelbarrow wobbled dangerously, and Barny forgot all about the mysterious figures.

'Are you mad?' he hissed. 'If you wake Nan up, the whole plan's ruined.'

'Thought you said she'd sleep through a brass band,' said Spag.

'We don't want to push our luck.' Barny peered into the wheelbarrow. 'Have you got all the stuff there?'

Clipper nodded. 'There's *oceans* of it. We're never going to get it all fixed in time.'

'Course we are.' Barny grabbed a couple of the carrier bags and led the way into the yard. 'You can fix the bottles on, and Spag and I can put up the curtain.'

'Hmmph.' Spag didn't look delighted. 'Wouldn't you rather help Clipper?'

'No he wouldn't,' Clipper said quickly. 'I need to work *fast*. And his fingers are like bunches of bananas.' She looked across at the FutureScope. 'I'll never get this wheelbarrow through. Not past all that junk. We'll have to take the things out and carry them.'

'Give me the curtain.' Barny grabbed at the folded material in the wheelbarrow.

'No!' hissed Spag.

But it was too late. As Barny tugged, the cassette player came flying out of the folds of the curtain.

'Pinhead!' Clipper dived forward and caught the cassette player, just as it was about to hit the ground.

Spag heaved a loud sigh of relief. 'Thanks, Clip. I thought that had had it. I'd never be able to buy my mum another one.'

Clipper dusted it off with her sleeve. She grinned. 'I don't suppose you would. It's a real antique, isn't it?'

Spag grinned back, but Barny was distracted. As Clipper said *a real antique*, he thought he heard something outside. Voices. Whispering.

'Hey – ' he muttered.

But Clipper wasn't going to stand around and chat. 'Save it till tomorrow, Gobbo. We've got to get going.'

Picking up Spag's plastic bags, she began to wade across the yard, past the tiles and the basins and the fireplaces.

'Hold out your arms, Gobbo,' said Spag. 'And be careful with these things. They're *precious*.'

Barny stretched out his hands – and stopped. Just for a second, he had heard them again. The whispers.

'Spag – '

But Spag was as brisk as Clipper. 'We'd better not talk too much. In case we wake your nan. Just take these.'

He loaded Barny with the things from the wheelbarrow and the two of them followed Clipper. She was already standing by the FutureScope, studying one of Spag's diagrams.

'This is dead complicated,' she muttered. 'It'll take an hour to fix each one.'

'Of course it won't. Look, this is how it goes.' Spag picked up a bottle and he and Clipper disappeared round the far side of the water tank.

Barny unfolded the curtain and draped it

carefully over the opening of the Future-Scope. The material caught on the rough metal edge at the top and hung down in long, straight folds.

Suddenly, he felt hopeful. After all those weeks of modelling and planning and hiding, things were starting to happen. The Future-Scope was going to work! Picking up the torch that Spag and Clipper had brought, he lifted the curtain and crawled inside the tank.

It was dark when the curtain fell back into place, and it would be even darker once the pipe holes were all covered by bottles. Barny turned on the torch and shone it down the pipe where Spag and Clipper were fixing the first bottle.

It was like looking down a telescope at tiny people, far away. He could see two mini-villains, with black masks over their faces and axes in their hands. And three policemen, parachuting down to arrest the villains and save the trees. It all looked so real that he held his breath. For a moment, as the torch shook and the shadows flickered, he almost expected the figures to move.

'What are you doing in there, Gobbo?' Clipper called, down another pipe. 'Are you lounging about? We can't afford to waste time, you know.'

'Course I'm not lounging about. I'm just going to put the notices up inside.'

Barny crawled out of the FutureScope and began hunting for the first notice. The one that said *What will the worst crime be in a hundred years' time?*

'I'll tell you what,' he said as he rummaged. 'It's even better than we thought. It's going to look like – like a million dollars.'

Clipper nodded. 'No chance of the school being closed down because it's old-fashioned. I bet this'll be enough to save it, all on its own.'

On the other side of the wall, there was a sudden, loud gasp.

'Wow!'

This time they all heard the voice.

'There's someone there!' hissed Spag. 'Someone's listening to us!'

Clipper dived towards the gate, weaving in and out of the heaps of junk, at top speed. But she was too late. In a second or two she was back, shaking her head.

'Don't know who it was, but they've gone now. I was just in time to see them nip round the corner.'

'Do you think – ?' Barny began.

'What's the point in talking about it?' said Spag. 'We don't know who it was. It could have been anyone. Probably just people walking past.'

Clipper nodded. 'That's right. We can't waste time thinking. We've got things to *do*.'

'But – ' Barny said.

Clipper and Spag ignored him and began fixing bottles again. Still frowning, Barny picked up the heap of notices and went back into the FutureScope.

It took them an hour to fix all the bottles and get the cassette player to work. And then there was the painting to do.

'Gobbo and me will do the patterns,' said Clipper. 'You ought to do the letters, Spag. You're the neatest.'

Spag nodded and picked up a paintbrush. 'Every letter a different colour. OK?'

Clipper nodded and began to paint a space station just beside the entrance.

By the time they had finished, it was hard to believe that the FutureScope had ever been a water tank. A bright red curtain hung down over the open front, and mysterious bottle shapes stuck out of the back and the sides. Stars and space ships were painted all round the edges and on each side Spag had written huge, multi-coloured words.

COME IN!
TAKE A PEEP AT THE FUTURE!
IF YOU DARE!

'It's brilliant!' Clipper said softly. 'It's pure gold. Let's each have a go before we go home.'

She took the torch and crawled through the curtain. Barny and Spag could hear her muttering the questions on the notices.

'Where will electricity come from?'

Then she shone the torch down the pipe. Spag nudged Barny as the first plastic bottle lit up. 'Look, you can see the shadows of the windmills.'

They followed round as Clipper read the other notices. When she got to *What pets will people have?* the pandas and tigers made beautiful shadows. So did the model of Bennett School when she reached *What danger will this school face?*

'But you can't see the flood from outside,' hissed Barny. 'I still think we should have had *real* water.'

'Don't be stupid.' Spag pointed at the next bottle. 'Might just as well say we should have had real sun for *What will the weather be like?*'

'That's not the same. The sunbathers are brilliant for showing how hot it's going to be. Especially with their sunhats and sunshades and tubes of suntan cream. But the water – '

'Oh shut up about the water,' Spag said impatiently. 'She's got to *What will be Top of the Pops?* and I want to hear if it works properly.'

It certainly did. As Clipper lifted the flap, they could see the shadows of four tiny figures with weird musical instruments. And at the same moment, their futuristic extraordinary, terrible song began echoing through the tank. It was stunning.

Too stunning. While they were still admiring it, a voice called from the house, even louder than the music.

'Barny? Whatever's the matter?'

It was his grandmother. She was standing in the doorway, peering into the dark yard.

'I'm all right,' Barny called back.

But it was no use saying that. 'How can you be all right?' yelled his grandmother. 'I can hear you groaning.'

It was true. Barny's deep, dreadful groans filled the yard. And his grandmother wasn't going to be put off.

'I'm sure there's something wrong. I'm coming to find you.'

Spag gave Barny a push. 'Quick! Say you're coming. But don't go too fast. We'll crawl to the gate, and you can lock it after us.'

Barny had one last, admiring look at the FutureScope. Then he yelled, 'Coming, Nan!'

Immediately, Clipper and Spag were off, like a pair of snakes crawling through long grass. While Barny was still squeezing his way round the fireplaces, they were at the gate.

Clipper grabbed the wheelbarrow as she passed it.

'Barny?' called his grandmother, peering harder into the darkness. 'Is that you over by the gate?'

'No, I'm here, Nan.'

As she turned to look at him, Spag and Clipper slipped through the gate and away. When Barny got to the gate, he could hear them chuckling as they pushed the wheel-barrow away up the road.

He knew just how they felt. Everything was going to be all right! The FutureScope was brilliant! Of course his mum and dad would be thrilled with it. Of course his dad would take it to school for them. And they'd win the prize . . . And . . .

Barny shut the gate firmly, and locked it. Then he hurried back to the house, before his nan could come snooping.

He had completely forgotten about the dark figures, and the whispers on the other side of the wall.

He was so impatient to show the FutureScope to his parents that he woke up an hour earlier than usual. When he looked at his clock, he saw that it was only six o'clock.

For ten minutes he lay in bed wondering how soon he could speak to them. Then he heard his mother get up and go down to the kitchen. Quickly he slid out of bed and fol-lowed her.

'Thought you were tired,' she said, when he appeared in the doorway. 'You ought to go back and have another hour.'

'I – ' Barny slid his finger up and down the door frame. 'It's Anniversary Day today.'

'So? You still need your sleep.'

'Yes, but – ' Barny hesitated. He wanted to tell her about the FutureScope without making her angry, but he wasn't quite sure how to do it. 'I – er – what's Dad doing this morning?'

'Going to Sheffield to pick up a load of metal posts. He's off in half an hour.' Barny's face fell, and she looked at him sharply. 'Why d'you want to know?'

'Because – um – ' Barny crossed his fingers behind his back ' – because we need him to help us take our project to school. In the lorry. It's – ' he crossed his fingers harder ' – it's rather big and heavy.'

'Is it indeed?' Mrs Gobbo sniffed. But she hadn't said *No* yet. Barny began to feel hopeful. 'And where is this big, heavy project?'

'It's – ' Barny gulped. 'It's in the yard.'

Mrs Gobbo stopped smiling. Before she could say anything, Barny was tugging her towards the window.

'You've got to come and look and you'll see how brilliant it is. No one's going to have anything like it, and it's sure to be in the Exhibition and win the prize, and that's what you said you wanted, and – '

He grabbed the curtain with his other hand and hauled it open. 'Look!'

There was a pause.

'Well?' Mrs Gobbo said heavily. 'Where is it then?'

'It's – '

Barny waved a hand towards the window and stopped suddenly, with his mouth falling open. The yard was still shut, with the gates tightly padlocked, but over on the far side, beyond the tiles and the basins, was a large empty space.

The FutureScope had gone.

7

On the Trail

Barny whirled round. 'What's happened to it? What's Dad done with it?'

'What's Dad done with what?' Mrs Gobbo looked baffled.

'With that big old water tank that was in the corner of the yard.'

Mrs Gobbo frowned. 'That's funny. It was there when we got back from darts. I know it was, because it looked a bit strange in the dark. As if it had lumps on the sides.'

'They were *our* lumps,' Barny said. 'What *happened* to them?'

'Nothing happened. Dad took Nan home and then he locked up the yard, same as usual.'

'But the tank's gone!' Barny said frantically. 'All our project was in it. We spent weeks and weeks working on it. And now someone's stolen it!'

'Why would anyone want to steal an old tank?' Mrs Gobbo shook her head. 'And even if they did, how could they get it out with the gates shut?'

'But it's *gone!*' Barny couldn't see why his mother was being so stupid. What did it matter *how* the FutureScope had been taken? The important thing was to find it.

He bounded towards the kitchen door.

'*Oh* no,' Mrs Gobbo said firmly. 'Not without dressing. And washing.' She grabbed him by the scruff of the neck and hauled him back.

'But what's the point of washing while the criminals are getting away?'

'And don't forget to do behind your ears.'

'*Mum!*'

'The sooner you're ready, the sooner you'll be able to get out.'

Barny tore upstairs into the bathroom. He scrubbed his neck and his face and his ears and his teeth, and any other bits that he could think of. Then he raced into his bedroom and pulled on all his clothes, at top speed. But it was still almost half-past six by the time he got downstairs again.

'Don't you want any breakfast?' his mother said.

'Course I don't. This is *serious*.'

He grabbed the yard key off its hook by the back door and ran out to undo the padlock on the yard gates. Perhaps somehow the FutureScope had got outside. Perhaps it was on the pavement.

But when he threw the gates open, all he found outside was Spag and Clipper. They beamed at him.

'We came early,' Clipper said. 'We wanted to see your mum and dad's faces when they saw the FutureScope.'

'And we wanted to help load it on to the lorry,' said Spag.

'We won't *be* loading it on to the lorry,' Barny said grimly.

'Why not?' Clipper grabbed his arm.

'Because it's gone!' He stepped back to let them in, and then pointed across the yard. 'Look!'

They glanced over to the corner and stared.

'Where is it?' Spag said at last. 'Has your father moved it?'

Barny shook his head. 'It's just gone.'

'We can see it's gone, pinbrain,' said Clipper. 'But *where* has it gone?'

'I don't know. Nor does my mum. She says it was here when they locked up last night. And no one's broken in. And there wasn't any noise. But it's gone.'

'Hmm.' Spag whipped out his notebook. 'A mystery. We'd better look for clues.'

He led the way to the corner where they had left the FutureScope the night before, and they began to hunt. They walked round and round the empty space where the tank had been. They peered at the ground. They poked into all the heaps of junk round about. But they didn't find a thing.

'There's not even a *mark*,' Barny said, frowning. 'If it had been carried out, the corners would have scraped all sorts of things.'

'No one could have *got* it out,' Spag said. 'Not without shifting all the tiles and basins and fireplaces first. And none of them have been moved, except where Mrs Potter fell over. You can tell by the dust.'

'It must have gone somewhere!' said Clipper impatiently. 'It can't just have flown away.'

Spag's eyes lit up suddenly. He took a step backwards and looked up at the top of the wall. Then he grinned.

'Clip, you're a genius!'

'Ha, ha, ha,' muttered Clipper.

'No really. Look.' Spag pointed up at the top of the wall. 'See that scrape? It looks really bright and new. I reckon the thieves must have lifted the whole thing over the wall.'

'They must have been very strong,' Clipper said doubtfully. 'And why would anyone go to all that bother, just to steal our FutureScope?'

Barny opened his mouth. And then shut it again. He remembered the whispers they'd heard on the other side of the wall. And he thought of a person who was longing to get his hands on the FutureScope. Someone who thought it was filled with valuable antiques. But that was ridiculous. Thrasher could never have lifted the FutureScope over the wall.

Spag was scribbling busily. 'That's one good clue we've found. Let's go outside and see if there are any more.'

They headed for the gates. When they were halfway there, a voice bellowed from the kitchen window. 'You're not leaving this yard until you've got some breakfast inside you!'

Barny looked back over his shoulder. 'Aw, Mum! This is important!'

'So is breakfast. You wait there until I come.'

A minute later, Mrs Gobbo came bursting through the back door with her hands full. 'Bacon sandwiches. One for each of you.'

'Scrummy!' Clipper went to meet her. '*And* they're still warm. You're a genius, Mrs Gobbo. Thanks a lot.'

'Hmm.' Mrs Gobbo looked sharply at them. Then she looked at the empty space by the wall and nodded briskly. 'I hope you work out where it went.'

'So do I,' Barny said grimly. 'Come on, you two.'

Chewing hard, the three of them went through the gate.

'Now,' said Spag, peering down at his

notes. 'If we go along the wall until we're level with the – ?'

'Look!'

Clipper darted ahead and bent down to examine the road. 'There's a lot of mud here.'

Barny went to inspect it. 'And tyre marks. Someone's been turning round.'

'Of course they have!' Clipper almost shook him. 'There's been a lorry turning here. It picked up the FutureScope and then it turned round and drove off.'

Spag came and peered at the marks too. Taking a ruler out of his pocket, he measured the width of the tyre and then he sketched the pattern on a clean page of his notebook.

'That's another good clue,' Barny said. 'But it's going to take a lot of hard work to find the lorry. We'll have to go looking at tyres and measuring wheels and – '

'No we won't!' Clipper was so impatient now that she was jumping up and down. 'All we've got to do is follow the marks.'

'Follow the – ?' Spag looked up from his notebook and Barny turned round. Then they both grinned. Because it was easy to see where the lorry had gone. As it drove away up the road, it had scattered bits of mud everywhere.

'Come on!' Clipper started up the road and looked back to see if the others were following her. 'We've got to go now. Before the mud gets scattered and moved.'

Barny looked at the mud again. 'We don't know *who's* taken the FutureScope, do we? They might be dangerous criminals.'

'Don't be so soft, Gobbo.' Clipper grabbed Barny's arm. 'We've got to find it before school. Come on.'

It was no use arguing. They were on the trail and they all had to follow it together. Away they went, keeping their eyes down, fixed on the road, so that they didn't miss anything.

They didn't have far to go. The muddy tracks went round a couple of corners, along the High Street and down the side road that led to the new shopping centre.

And there they had to stop. The new shopping centre wasn't finished yet. It was just a muddy building site with a high wooden fence all round it. And the tracks led up to the gate in the fence.

'The lorry went in there.' Clipper rattled the door, but it was locked. 'What do we do now? Wait here for it to come out again?'

Spag frowned. 'We could wait for *hours*. They won't start work until half-past eight. And we don't even know it's the right lorry, do we? We only guessed.'

He and Clipper began to walk round in circles, studying the muddy tyre marks as if they were a secret code. But Barny was bored with mud. He wandered off along the fence, trying to find a crack to look through.

But the fence was very solid. After two or three minutes, he gave it up as a bad job. Turning round, he started to walk back to Clipper and Spag.

And that was when he looked up for the first time.

'Hey!' he yelled. 'Stop staring at the road! Look *up!*'

'What are you on about?' Clipper said. 'Look up where?'

'Look up in the sky! You said the tank must have vanished into the sky and you were right!'

'Stop fooling about, Gobbo.' Spag straightened up. '*I* don't think it's funny.'

Then Clipper gave a great hoot of laughter. 'Oh yes it is! Gobbo's right! Look up, Spag!'

Spag turned and his mouth fell open. Way above their heads, on the other side of the fence, was a large crane lorry. And hanging from the arm of the crane, high in the air, was the FutureScope.

They were still gazing up, when there was a sound on the other side of the gate. Footsteps and then a key in the lock. The gate flew open.

Suddenly, they found themselves staring straight at Thrasher.

For a second, he looked as startled as they did. Then his face twisted with fury.

'Suppose you think you're *really clever*, don't you? Conning me like that. Bet you've been splitting your sides because I believed all those lies about antiques.'

'We never said anything about antiques,' said Clipper. 'You were the one who made all that up.'

Thrasher gritted his teeth. 'Made it up, did I? Well, why did you keep going on about how *valuable* the stuff was?' He waved a hand back at the crane and the dangling Future-Scope. 'It's nothing but a rotten old tank with lots of polythene bottles and silly little

116

models. Windmills and houses and *dear* little cuddly pandas.'

'It *is* valuable to us,' Spag said.

'Oh sure,' sneered Thrasher. 'And I suppose you weren't trying to make a fool of me?'

'You don't need anyone to make a fool of you,' Clipper snapped. 'You can do it all by yourself.'

'Grrr!'

Thrasher gritted his teeth and flung himself at Clipper, with his fists flying. She charged to meet him, ready to give as good as she got. But before the fight could get properly started, someone else came through the gate.

One huge hand fell on Clipper's collar. The other fell on Thrasher's. They were lifted right off the ground and put down well away from each other.

'So what's going on here?' said Tiny Dyson.

Barny took a deep breath. 'Nothing's going on. We just want our FutureScope back.'

'Hmm.' Tiny looked up at the crane. Then he looked down, thoughtfully, at Barny, Spag and Clipper. 'That thing of yours has caused me a lot of trouble. *Someone's* been giving Thrasher very peculiar ideas about it.'

'It wasn't just me,' Thrasher said sulkily. 'You heard them too, Tiny. They said it was precious, didn't they? A real antique. They said it was worth enough to save their mouldy old school, all by itself.'

'So it was you on the other side of the wall last night?' said Spag. 'Listening to us.'

'But we didn't mean we had *real* antiques?' Barny looked round helplessly. How could he possibly explain?

'The FutureScope's not worth a bean,' Clipper said. 'Except to us. It's our project for the school Anniversary Day competition.'

'The Anniversary Day competition . . .'

Barny, Spag and Clipper didn't dare to look at each other as Tiny Dyson repeated the words. What would he do? Would he fly into a rage?

He went on brooding for a moment or two. Then a slow smile spread across his face. 'Well, now, I reckon we owe you an apology.'

'Yes you do!' said Clipper.

Barny kicked her. She never knew when to be tactful. 'That's quite all right,' he said politely. 'But we would like our FutureScope back. Because it's Anniversary Day today.'

Tiny went on grinning. 'Course you would. Course you want it back. How about if I deliver it for you?'

Barny could hardly believe his ears. Did Tiny really mean it? If he did, their problems were solved.

'Do you – would you – could you possibly take it to the school for us?'

118

'Of course I can. No hassle. Just stand back while I fetch out my crane.'

Barny looked up at the crane and gave a sigh of relief. 'Oh, you *work* here.'

'Not any more I don't. They gave me the push last Friday.' Tiny grinned again, and waved a piece of bent wire at them. 'But it doesn't take much to fix these locks. And I reckon they owe me a favour. Come on, Thrash.'

The two Dysons marched into the yard and climbed up into the crane. A few seconds later, it was lumbering across the building site towards them, with the FutureScope swinging in its grab.

'Off we go, then!' called Tiny. 'To the Bennett School!'

He turned the crane into the road and Barny, Clipper and Spag began to run along behind, trying to keep up.

'Wasn't I brilliant?' panted Barny. 'To think of getting him to deliver it?'

'I don't like it.' Clipper shook her head as she jogged beside Barny. 'The day those Dysons turn nice is the day the moon goes purple. What are they up to?'

'We'll find out soon enough,' gasped Spag. 'We'll be there in a moment. If they really are taking it there.'

Suppose they weren't? Barny hadn't thought of that. Suppose the crane just went sailing past the school?

But it didn't. It slowed and came to a stop neatly outside the front door. Tiny leaned out of the cab.

'Where d'you want it, then?'

Barny looked up at the FutureScope,

swinging in midair. Then he looked at the school. 'Could you put it down in the yard? Just on the other side of the railings?'

'I certainly can.' Tiny looked sideways at Thrasher and the two of them grinned at each other.

'They won't do it!' Clipper hissed into Barny's ear. 'They'll drive off suddenly, just when we think they're going to put it down.'

But they didn't do that either. Inside the cab, Tiny spun the wheel and the crane turned until its arm was pointing over the railings, into the school's front yard.

'Here?'

'That's great,' yelled Barny. 'Thanks a lot!'

He waited for the lifting arm to dip, lowering the FutureScope on to the ground. But it didn't. Instead Tiny grinned and whispered something to Thrasher. Then he pulled a lever.

The grab opened, high in the air. And the FutureScope went crashing to the ground.

8

Anniversary Day

For a moment there was no sound except the clang of metal and the clatter of plastic. Then Tiny Dyson chuckled.

'Oh dear. How clumsy of me.'

'You – you – ' Barny clenched his fists and

gritted his teeth. 'We spent *hours* working on that. And now it's ruined.'

'Boo hoo hoo.' Thrasher rubbed his eyes. 'All your dear little cuddly things are spoilt, are they?'

Clipper turned her back on the crane. 'Don't talk to them,' she said.

Spag turned his back as well and folded his arms. But Barny hesitated. He wanted to scream and shout at Thrasher and Tiny. He wanted to report them to the police. He wanted –

Clipper grabbed his shoulders and turned him round by force. 'Ignore them! The more fuss we make, the more they'll like it.'

Reluctantly, Barny shut his mouth and folded his arms. And after a few seconds it worked. With a graunching, grinding noise, Tiny backed the crane away from the school.

'Got no time to stay and chatter to you kids. Have to get this crane back, before they start work on the site. So long, suckers!'

'Happy Anniversary!' yelled Thrasher, grinning and waving.

As the crane disappeared round the corner, Barny, Spag and Clipper stood side by side, gloomily peering through the railings.

'It's completely ruined,' muttered Barny.

Spag nodded. 'All the plastic bottles are off. And split. And I bet the models are smashed to pieces.'

'After all that work,' groaned Barny.

'Don't give up yet!' Clipper said fiercely. 'I'm going to see how bad it is. Give us a leg-up, Spag.'

Spag hoisted her up and she clambered over the railings and dropped down into the yard. The other two watched as she prowled round, collecting up plastic bottles and lifting the curtain to peer inside the FutureScope.

When she came to the railings she was looking even gloomier than Spag and Barny.

'It's pretty bad. Look.'

She turned a couple of the plastic bottles upside down and shook them. There was a dull rattle and little pieces of wood and card-board scattered over the ground.

'You see? They're all like that. And the torch is smashed. And I think the cassette player's broken, too. Nothing happened when I tried the switch.'

Spag pulled a terrible face. 'Hmmph. I borrowed that from my mum. And I didn't exactly tell her. I thought she wouldn't mind when she saw how brilliant the FutureScope was.

'Nobody's ever going to see how brilliant it was,' said Clipper mournfully. 'The tank's OK. So's the curtain. And we can easily fix the notices back. But there's no point in lifting them, because there's nothing to see.'

'What good is a FutureScope that doesn't let you *see* anything?' said Spag.

Barny felt a strange prickling at the back of his neck. It was almost like the beginning of an idea . . .

Spag and Clipper went on talking.

'It all looked so good last night.'

'But no one saw it. Only us.'

'They'll never believe how lifelike all those little people looked. Under the lights and everything.'

It LOOKED so good. No one SAW it . . . the little people LOOKED lifelike . . . Inside Barny's head the idea grew and grew.

'We'll get into trouble with Mr Fox, too,' Clipper went on crossly. 'He'll think we never did a project.'

Spag nodded miserably. 'And Soppy Elaine will say she was right all along, won't she?'

'And Spotty will probably invent another new word about us. Won't he, Gobbo?'

'Hmm.' Barny hardly heard them. He was too busy thinking up the details of his idea. Clipper whirled round and shook him.

'Why don't *you* say something, Gobbo? Or don't you care about the FutureScope?'

'What?' Barny blinked. 'Of course I care about it. It was my idea, wasn't it?' He took a deep breath, ready to stun them with his brilliant *new* idea. But before he could get started, Clipper interrupted him.

'It may have been your idea, but I made the models. And – '

'And I did the diagrams,' broke in Spag. 'And I found – '

Clipper elbowed him in the ribs. 'Well, I thought up half the ideas for the peepholes – '

'I worked out the scientific bits!' Spag said indignantly. 'And – '

'I worked for hours and hours – '

'I practically *lived* in the library – '

'I – '

Barny put his hands over his ears and yelled at them. 'WILL YOU TWO SHUT UP?'

Spag and Clipper stopped and stared.

'No need to make a fuss,' said Clipper.

'We're not hurting you,' said Spag.

Barny glared at them. 'You're wasting *time*. If we're going to get the FutureScope fixed before the beginning of school, we need to get going.'

Clipper gave him a pitying look. 'We haven't got a hope of fixing all those models. It would take weeks.'

'I'm not talking about the models,' Barny said impatiently. 'We'd never get those done in time. I've got a new plan.'

Clipper looked at him doubtfully. 'Spit it out, then.'

'Well – all those models – they're all things you *see*, aren't they?'

Spag gave him a puzzled look. 'Of course

they are. That's what peepholes are for. Looking at things.'

'But suppose our peepholes are different,' Barny said slowly. 'Suppose you don't see things through them. Suppose you *hear* things or *smell* things or *feel* things?'

'Gobbo,' Clipper said, 'you've gone off your rocker.'

'No I haven't! Lend us your notebook, Spag.'

With the other two watching, Barny wrote down the list of things he had been putting together in his head.

bellows	hot water bottle
porridge	plastic bucket
musical box	waterweed
burnt wood	pepper
teddy bear	blue cheese
dirty socks	nettles

Clipper groaned. 'I was right. You're complete nutty, Gobbo.'

'No I'm not.' Barny grinned, annoyingly. 'If we can get all these things, we can make a FutureScope that's worth going into. What can you bring?'

'I'll bring my breakfast,' Spag said promptly. 'Any excuse not to eat my mum's porridge. And we've got a pair of bellows, too. They're in the fireplace.'

Clipper read the list again. 'I can bring the wood. Dad had a bonfire yesterday. And the dirty socks. There are *billions* of those on my brothers' floor. And Mum'll let me have some pepper and blue cheese. But why – ?'

Barny didn't let her finish. 'We've got to get going,' he said firmly. 'There's no time to waste. You two bring the things you've promised, and I'll find the rest. But don't let people see you, or it'll spoil the surprises.'

'If people see us, they'll think we've gone loony,' Clipper muttered. But she ran off towards her house muttering the list of things she had to find. 'Dirty socks, pepper, blue cheese . . .'

★

By the time Barny got back to school, everyone else was arriving too. As he came round
the corner, clutching his bag of strange
things, he saw dozens of children marching
up the road.

Spotty was tottering under the weight of
his *New Improved Expanded Dictionary of
Twenty-First Century Slang*. Sharon Grove
was mincing along behind him with her hair
looped and piled and twisted into the most
extraordinary style. And Elaine was just
arriving in her mother's car.

Mrs Potter opened the back door and
Elaine slid out of the car like a film star.

'I couldn't walk,' she simpered. 'In case it
rained on my hair.' She patted her clustered,
entwined ringlets and smiled graciously as
Sharon came up. 'Your hair's lovely too,
Sharon. Nearly as good as mine.'

The two of them posed and preened themselves on the pavement while Mrs Potter took
a large suitcase out of the car.

'Our clothes for The Exhibition,' Soppy
Elaine informed everyone in a loud voice.
'They're fabulous. Just *wait* till you see them.'

'Mcgrew,' muttered Spotty sarcastically.
'Have you got fabulous clothes in your bag
too, Clip?'

Clipper was marching up the road with a
bulging carrier bag. She grinned as she
reached them.

'I've got some clothes, but they're not exactly fabulous. They're my brothers' socks.'

'Eugh!' The smile disappeared from Soppy Elaine's face. 'They smell *disgusting!*'

Clipper held out the bag. 'Want to take a look?'

'Certainly not!' Soppy Elaine backed away as fast as she could. 'I don't want to pick up your smells. I've had a bath, with bath oil and washed my hair specially with *very expensive shampoo*.'

'Good scheme,' murmured Spotty. 'Hiding your own smell with something better. *Potterflage*.'

He pulled out a pen to add the word to his dictionary. But then he saw Soppy Elaine's mother looking at him, so he put it away again.

Soppy Elaine sniffed. 'Come on, Sharon. Don't take any notice of *him*. We've got to go into school and get ready. For when the Head Mister comes round to give The Prize.'

Mrs Potter beamed and handed her the suitcase. 'I'll be along straight after lunch. As soon as it's open to the public. I'm looking forward to seeing you.'

Soppy Elaine and Sharon swept across the yard and into school. As they passed the ruined FutureScope, Soppy Elaine gave a dramatic shudder. 'I hope someone takes that *terrible* junk away before The Exhibition. It will make such a bad impression on The Public.'

She led Sharon into the school, and Spotty followed. Barny beckoned Clipper.

'We've got to get going. Did you find everything I said?'

Clipper nodded. 'How about you?'

'Everything except the teddy bear.' Barny grinned. 'I had a better idea afterwards. *Much* better.'

But there was no time to explain. They had to be ready by the time the Head Mister came round. Barny started giving Clipper instructions.

'Stuff the dirty socks in – let me see – yes, into this pipe. And put the pepper in this one. And the blue cheese in here.'

While she was doing that, he pushed his own things into pipes and hung the bucket in place. With its handle over the top pipe, its rim was just level with the next pipe down. Barny tied a piece of string round it and threaded that through the lower pipe.

The bucket tipped beautifully.

'Go and get some water, Clip,' he said.

'Honestly, Gobbo, I wish you'd *explain*.'

But Barny had no time. Spag was just walking through the gate and he had to be told what to do with his things.

'Porridge here. No, we don't want the plate.

131

Tip it right into the pipe. And the bellows here. One of us will have to stand there and work them. There's no time to rig up a switch.'

'But – '

Barny didn't explain to Spag, either. Instead, he picked up Clipper's burnt wood and sniffed it.

'Brilliant,' he said. 'It smells of burnt wood.'

He stuffed it into one of the pipes and then ducked inside the FutureScope. Pulling out a felt pen, he began to add words to the notices.

WHERE WILL WE GET ELECTRICITY FROM? – FEEL!

WHAT WILL THE MOST POPULAR FOOD BE? – TASTE!

WHAT WILL BE TOP OF THE POPS? – PULL STRING!

WHAT WILL THE WORST CRIME BE? – SMELL!

HOW WILL WE DEAL WITH GLOBAL WARMING? – FEEL!

WHAT WILL HOUSES BE LIKE? – SMELL!

WHAT WILL BE THE BEST WAY TO TRAVEL? – SMELL!

WHAT WILL THE WEATHER BE LIKE? – FEEL!

WHAT DANGER WILL THIS SCHOOL FACE – PULL STRING!

WHAT SUN PROTECTION WILL WE USE? – FEEL!

WHAT WILL PEOPLE DO AT SCHOOL? – SMELL!
WHAT WILL BE THE MOST POPULAR PET? –
FEEL!

He had just finished when Clipper rapped sharply on the side of the tank.

'Gobbo! He's here!'

Then another voice spoke. A deep and rather puzzled voice. 'And what exactly are you doing?'

The Head Mister!

Barny crawled out of the FutureScope and stood up. 'Er – hallo, sir. Er . . . this is our project. It's not quite finished. There's one more little bit to do.'

The Head stood for a moment examining the battered FutureScope. In spite of its dents, it still looked bright and lively, and Spag's letters were still clear.

COME IN!
TAKE A PEEP AT THE FUTURE!!
IF YOU DARE!!!

'Hmm,' said the Head. 'Shall I take a look?'

'I – um – '

Before Barny could think what to say, the Head bent down and crawled into the FutureScope.

'What are we going to do?' hissed Spag. 'We can't do all those things to him.'

133

'We *must!*' Barny pushed Spag into place.
'Get ready to work the bellows.'

'You mean *I've got to blow air into the Head
Mister's face?*'

'Yes!' Barny said firmly. 'Get ready!'

Spag was only just in time. The Head had already begun to read out the first notice.

'Where will we get our electricity from?' said his muffled voice from inside the FutureScope.

'Now!' Barny and Clipper hissed, as he lifted the flap.

Spag pumped the bellows and sent a jet of air down the pipe. For a moment there was a startled silence inside the FutureScope.

Then the Head Mister roared with laughter. 'Oh very good. Wind power. I think you're right. I think there will be lots of wind parks. What's the next one? *What will be the most popular pet?*'

'I haven't done that one yet,' Barny called. 'Go on to the one after. Where you have to taste the most popular food.'

'What is it?' whispered Clipper.

Barny grinned. 'Cold porridge.'

'But you're not going to let – '

'Ssh!'

'EUGH!' said the Head from inside. Then he laughed again.

He seemed to enjoy all the peepholes. He laughed very loudly when he got to *What will be the most popular way to travel?* That was the pipe with Clipper's brothers' socks in.

'No doubt about that!' he murmured. 'Feet!'

And he liked the *Top of the Pops* one too.

When he pulled the string, Barny's musical box played 'I'm Dreaming of a White Christmas'.

'That's right,' they heard him say. 'It will be just a dream by then.'

But Barny was waiting for him to reach the last peephole. When he did, he sounded even more interested.

'Oh, I've got to try this. I need to know about dangers to the school.'

'It's not the bucket, is it?' hissed Clipper.

Barny nodded. 'Of course it is. The school's in danger of flooding, isn't it?'

The three of them watched as the Head pulled the string. Slowly, the bucket tilted and a stream of water poured into the pipe.

There was a splutter from inside. Then the Head appeared, brushing water off his jacket. But he was grinning.

'You're not cross?' said Clipper.

'Certainly not.' The Head looked over his shoulder at the FutureScope. 'It's funny and exciting but it's serious too. You've all spent a lot of time thinking about how things might change, haven't you?'

'Well – ' said Barny.

'Yes!' said Spag. 'I spent hours in the library.'

'It shows,' said the Head. 'This is a thoughtful, lively project. The best I've seen.'

'You mean – ' Barny's eyes opened wide.

The Head grinned. 'Wait and see what I mean. You must come inside and look at all the others. Some of them are very good too.'

Clipper and Spag nodded and started towards the school, but Barny suddenly remembered something.

'I'll catch you up,' he called. 'I've just got to fill the last pipe.'

By the time the exhibition was due to open, dozens of people were standing outside the gates. When Spag and Clipper came back to find Barny, they saw Mrs Potter elbowing her way to the front of the queue.

'Elaine and Sharon will be the stars of this exhibition,' she was saying. 'They both look charming in their clothes. And of course they were really *clever* to design them. Especially Elaine. I'll be surprised if anyone else has done anything as good – '

'Hmmph,' said Mrs Gobbo. When Mrs Potter got to her, she stood firm.

Barny jumped up and down and waved his hands. 'Look, Mum, we found it! This is our project!'

'Well done, boy.' Mrs Gobbo smiled at him. 'I'll be in to see what you've done in a moment.'

'I've seen it already,' said a voice from the back of the queue. 'It's rubbish!'

Thrasher pushed his way through the

crowd, closely followed by three other King's Road boys.

'We've been sent from our school. To report on this exhibition.' He grinned at his friends. 'And it looks like a load of junk so far. Doesn't it?'

Before anyone could reply, the Head appeared. He came out of the school just in time to hear what Thrasher said and a smile flitted across his face.

'Ah yes,' he murmured. 'Mr Willoughby told me you boys were coming. Would you like to demonstrate the FutureScope for us?'

Thrasher snorted. 'I'll demonstrate what a load of garbage it is,' he muttered.

The Head Mister smiled again, but he didn't say anything. He just watched, as Thrasher pushed the gate open and headed for the FutureScope.

As he lifted the curtain and went inside, everyone fell silent, waiting to hear what would happen. They heard him read out the first notice.

'*What will the most popular pet be? Feel.* Oh har har. How sweet. Got another little furry thing, have you?'

'What *have* we got?' muttered Clipper.

Barny put his finger to his lips. 'Wait,' he mouthed.

'Cutchy, cutchy, cutchy coo,' jeered

Thrasher's voice. 'Are you in there, little furry thing?'

A second later, there was an incredible, disgusted yelp. Thrasher came shooting out of the FutureScope, shaking his right hand and rubbing at it, as if he were trying to get something off.

'Eugh! *EUGH!* It's foul! It's disgusting! It *moved!*'

He raced straight out of the school gates and away down the road.

'What is it?' Clipper hissed into Barny's ear.

'Nothing,' Barny said, innocently. 'Just some nice, small pets. Don't bite or sting. Very cheap to feed.'

'But what *are* they?' said Spag.

Barny grinned. 'Dear little cuddly – slugs.'

The Head was just taking a card out of his pocket. 'Hmmph,' he muttered, when he heard what Barny said. Pulling out a pen, he wrote a few words. Then he walked across to the FutureScope and propped the card on its roof.

'Well done, you three!' he said loudly. 'This is a fine project.'

Mrs Potter's mouth fell open, and her face went white. Mrs Gobbo nodded quietly at Barny, her eyes gleaming.

Printed on the card were the words

FIRST PRIZE

and underneath the Head had written, in black felt pen

(ENTER AT YOUR OWN RISK)

Clipper and Spag gave a yell of triumph.
'You've done it, Gobbo!' shouted Clipper.
'You're no fool!' said Spag.

Barny looked at the notice. Then he turned to look at Thrasher, who was still running down the road, as fast as he could go. A huge grin spread across his face.

'Of course I'm not a fool,' he said modestly. 'I'm GREAT!'

A Selected List of Fiction from Mammoth

While every effort is made to keep prices low, it is sometimes necessary to increase prices at short notice. Mammoth Books reserves the right to show new retail prices on covers which may differ from those previously advertised in the text or elsewhere.

The prices shown below were correct at the time of going to press.

☐	416 13972 8	**Why the Whales Came**	Michael Morpurgo £2.50
☐	7497 0034 3	**My Friend Walter**	Michael Morpurgo £2.50
☐	7497 0035 1	**The Animals of Farthing Wood**	Colin Dann £2.99
☐	7497 0136 6	**I Am David**	Anne Holm £2.50
☐	7497 0139 0	**Snow Spider**	Jenny Nimmo £2.50
☐	7497 0140 4	**Emlyn's Moon**	Jenny Nimmo £2.25
☐	7497 0344 X	**The Haunting**	Margaret Mahy £2.25
☐	416 96850 3	**Catalogue of the Universe**	Margaret Mahy £1.95
☐	7497 0051 3	**My Friend Flicka**	Mary O'Hara £2.99
☐	7497 0079 3	**Thunderhead**	Mary O'Hara £2.99
☐	7497 0219 2	**Green Grass of Wyoming**	Mary O'Hara £2.99
☐	416 13722 9	**Rival Games**	Michael Hardcastle £1.99
☐	416 13212 X	**Mascot**	Michael Hardcastle £1.99
☐	7497 0126 9	**Half a Team**	Michael Hardcastle £1.99
☐	416 08812 0	**The Whipping Boy**	Sid Fleischman £1.99
☐	7497 0033 5	**The Lives of Christopher Chant**	Diana Wynne-Jones £2.50
☐	7497 0164 1	**A Visit to Folly Castle**	Nina Beachcroft £2.25

All these books are available at your bookshop or newsagent, or can be ordered direct from the publisher. Just tick the titles you want and fill in the form below.

Mandarin Paperbacks, Cash Sales Department, PO Box 11, Falmouth, Cornwall TR10 9EN.

Please send cheque or postal order, no currency, for purchase price quoted and allow the following for postage and packing:

UK	80p for the first book, 20p for each additional book ordered to a maximum charge of £2.00.
BFPO	80p for the first book, 20p for each additional book.
Overseas including Eire	£1.50 for the first book, £1.00 for the second and 30p for each additional book thereafter.

NAME (Block letters) ....

ADDRESS ....

....

....